The Devil's Violin

By the author

Seven Visions and Other Poems
Silent House Publications / Los Angeles 1987
ISBN 0-942943-00-7

The Devil's Violin

Art Johnson

STORY MERCHANT BOOKS
BEVERLY HILLS / 2014

THE STORY
MERCHANT

http://www.art-johnson.com
http://www.wallmanproductions.com

Story Merchant Books
9601 Wilshire Boulevard #1202
Beverly Hills, CA 90210

http://www.storymerchant.com/books.html

Publisher's Note: This is a work of fiction. Names, characters, places, and incidents are a product of the author's imagination. Locales and public names are sometimes used for atmospheric purposes.
Any resemblance to actual people, living or dead, or to businesses, companies, events, institutions, or locales is completely coincidental.

Book design ©2014 Leslie Taylor, buffalocreativegroup.com

Beverly Hills / Art Johnson — First Edition

ISBN 978-0-9897154-6-1

Printed in the United States of America

For my sister, Judith

.

Prologue

When there is no hope for the future and the present is constant pain, then the past will absorb the soul searching for good things.
– Ancient Hindu proverb

*   *   *

A faint smile formed around the hollow cheeks of the bedridden man. Rain continued to slash the windows. This sound was transformed into melodies. Showers of ascending and descending notes flooded his consciousness. Crisp images embedded in memory arrived in rapid succession. The hundreds of concerts and the cities they were held in: women and the rooms he made love to them in. The money — oh yes, the millions he earned and lost in four decades.

He had jumped off the edge of the universe and changed the way the world would listen to music: the artist as prophet. With his singular imagination, he was shaping the future. The flow of sounds and textures would follow in his wake.

In his possession was a well guarded ritual passed down through the centuries by a chosen few: the artists, philosophers, writers, mathematicians, musicians and speculative scientists. The power of this manuscript, properly interpreted, had increased his musical vision. This document and scores similar to it were at the foundation of cultural, political and social change throughout the ages. Secret brotherhoods with one credo: to know, to dare, to be silent.

After re-inventing violin technique and performing with a personal passion beyond belief, audiences became suspicious. He appeared to be from another world. Many people were convinced that he was in league with the Devil. More than a few believed him to *be* the Devil. The image he had created for himself always caused him regret. It was impossible for anyone to understand the turmoil experienced in the process of making the invisible, audible.

Today his mind was at war with his body. He knew he was dying. In the darkness of his Mediterranean apartment a vampire was sucking the blood from his veins. Long, pointed finger nails scraping the marrow of his bones. Surely, God must be laughing.

Crawling out of bed with only the strength of his arms to aid him, he grabbed the knife from the table and crouched on the floor. His breathing was labored, but for the sake of his son he must finish what he'd begun three days ago. When Achilles returned with the doctor he would tell him the secret.

He removed the final plank of the flooring and inserted the violin case with the real 1742 Guarneri into the hiding spot, the instrument fashioned by the erratic genius of Cremona which had been his life-long companion: the voice which soared among the clouds.

Tucked behind the lining inside the case was the document he valued most dearly, translated from the original Latin into Italian and English: the magic formula of his success.

The ailing legend replaced the planks, making sure they looked untouched.

The copy of the Devil's violin he purchased in Paris a decade ago was on the bed. Last week, he had promised the real Guarneri to the mayor of Genoa, the city of his birth, for their museum. They would always believe the copy to be the original. His smile returned. The prophet knew that as time passed, the value of the original violin would increase a thousand fold. This unique instrument must be kept in the family.

*　　*　　*

Niccolo Paganini welcomed the new healer with little enthusiasm. He told his son that they would need to talk after the examination. There was no time for last words. One of the most mysterious personalities that ever lived, died within minutes of the doctor's arrival.

The next day, Achilles emptied his father's apartment and removed the body unaware of the treasure buried beneath the floor.

CHAPTER ONE

Emily Parker loved the older neighborhoods of Los Angeles. Tonight she was in one of her favorite 1920's mansions. She held up her half-empty martini, studying the image of two inverted triangles formed by the glass and its contents; an ancient alchemical symbol for the earth. The people around her enjoying Hollywood film producer Max Pendleton's party seemed to disappear. Her mind was elsewhere. The alcohol made her memory fuzzy around the edges yet the drug also allowed her to focus on the past. Not the decades that most people would review, but the deep past. Lifetimes of awareness experienced over centuries. Where would she be without Jonathan? He had rescued her during a time of political unrest when the Church and the populace were at war.

A voice came from over her shoulder. "Mrs. Parker?" Emily turned to discover a young man smiling at her. "I just had to meet the wife of Jonathan Parker."

She shifted slightly. "How do you know my husband?"

He pulled up a chair. "I've just started to work for Max. I've seen Mr. Parker before but only met him tonight. Wow, he's something else."

Emily stared into his face. "What's your name?"

He finished a sip of his Dewar's. "Roscoe, Roscoe Barnes."

"Well Roscoe, I agree with you, but why do you think so?"

Roscoe straightened his back. "We had a meeting a few minutes ago upstairs with our new Saudi clients. Your husband spoke Arabic. That blew my mind. We're working on a new investment deal. The sheiks want a piece of Hollywood."

Emily grabbed another martini off a passing tray. "Well young man, there are a lot of bilingual people floating around this village. It's not that big a deal."

Roscoe grinned. "Granted, but not many of them are investment geniuses who speak Arabic and play the violin like a god."

"Where did a violin come from?" Emily spilled a few drops of her drink.

Roscoe pretended not to notice. "You don't know about Max's collection? I didn't either until tonight, but upstairs behind a sliding panel are half a dozen old fiddles. Evidently they're worth a small fortune. Max was selling one and Jonathan played it. Incredible."

Emily asked Roscoe for a cigarette. He didn't smoke but said he would find her one. The martinis were taking effect. She began to laugh thinking about 'fat' Max with a violin. When Roscoe returned with a pack and a gold trimmed ash tray, he lit one for Emily and sat back down.

"There's one thing I just don't understand," Roscoe said with an exaggerated smile, "How in the hell does one man learn so much in one lifetime?"

Emily took a long drag of her cigarette. "Indeed, that is a curious thought worth examining."

She stared off into space and Roscoe, realizing she was finished with their conversation, stood up and moved back into the crowd of party makers.

CHAPTER TWO

Two

The boyish thief threw on his Ray-Bans as he stepped out into the summer sun along Santa Monica Boulevard. His meeting with Max was a tough one. The heists were getting more complex.

"People want what they want and don't give a shit how they get it." Gustav Edward Happy lit up a Camel and headed for his car. "Yep, and that's why I have a job."

Max paid well and Gus knew he'd be earning every penny on this new assignment. The job was in Europe and he'd never been farther than Las Vegas. "What the hell," he thought, "the Dodgers are on a losing streak — no reason to hang around."

The flight from LAX landed in Milan Monday morning. The sixty kilometers to Parma was travelled by train. Gus had experienced motion sickness since he was a kid. As the tundra of the Tuscan country side flew by two beers soothed his parched throat and kept him from puking.

It was the middle of August and Parma was empty. The sun beat down on the ancient cobblestones. There were no hordes of tourists.

His first day in Italy found Gus Happy alone in a small café waiting for his contact, someone named Mario. They were late. He fondled his espresso cup nervously while staring at the blue glow of his cell phone. A dry wind was blowing along the street reminding him of the Santa Ana's in L.A.

What the fuck had he gotten himself into this time? The feeling that someone had followed him from the train to his hotel yesterday was making him nervous. Two months ago he celebrated his fortieth birthday in Vegas. That night he'd felt on top of the world. Now it seemed that he was staring up from a dark ravine.

He ate but felt empty inside. Sitting on the terrace of the bistro with his back against the wall, he chain smoked. He checked his watch. He'd give it another fifteen minutes and then head back to the hotel. It was time to be cool. He knew his imagination could play tricks on him.

He was born into a family of thieves. The night he began his career, Uncle Eddy stopped by to take him for a drive. They drove around in a 1983 Lincoln town car. It was black, inside and out. The seats smelled like perfume. After a while Eddy veered down an alleyway in Tarzana and brought the car to a halt. He turned to Gus. "You know son, you've always been my favorite nephew. You've got brains." Between glances at his nephew, Eddy's eyes were darting around nervously. "Tell me, did you ever ask yourself what your father and I and your other uncle in Seattle do for a living?"

Before Gus could answer Eddy jerked open the driver's door and ran down the alley like an athlete. Gus stared at his uncle and another man as they disappeared around the corner.

Total silence.

His heart pounded like a drum. Was he imagining all of this…was it a dream? Would he wake up soon?

Gus jumped as he heard the sound of two gun shots crack in the air. Within a few seconds Uncle Eddy ambled back to the car sporting his big-toothed smile. Settling back in his seat he started the engine and handed Gus a Franklin. "Thanks for keeping me company. If you're interested there's more where this came from."

That had been the beginning. The past twenty three years rolled by in a blur. Nothing was distinguishable. His mind had wandered but he knew it was time to concentrate.

Thieves and poets have one quality in common: the trained faculty of observation. Gus could sense someone bearing down on him. His eyes scanned the street. To his left, two older women were walking, arm in arm, their heads bent in close to hear one another. On his right a beautiful woman was staring at him, smiling as if she were coming to greet a lover. She stopped in front of Gus and extended her right hand.

"You must be Gus," she said with an Italian accent. "I'm Maria, sorry to be a little late." Gus stumbled to his feet. He recognized her as the person who followed him from the train station. He moved around to offer her a chair. "Sorry, I was waiting for someone called Mario." He held out the note that the desk clerk had given him that morning.

"Oh Signor, in Italian the letter 'a' sometimes looks like an 'o'. Maria patted his cheek. "It is my fault. I should have been on time." She sat down crossing her olive colored legs. Her dress was simple, low cut, fitting her slender body without clinging to it. A crowned straw hat and huge oval sunglasses completed her statement. Gus thought of Sofia Loren.

He began to mentally size up his options before speaking. Maria ordered two more espressos. Due to his fatigue and anxiety Gus was spaced out. The last thing he had expected from Max was to hook him up with a female. "Well Maria, what's our next move?"

"You don't know?" Maria giggled as she spoke. Gus's cell phone went off. The sound was deafening in the empty plaza. Maria smiled at Gus. "You'd better answer it, it's probably Max."

Three

After a brief update with Gus, Max confirmed a few details with Maria and then locked away his untraceable cell phone. The tension in Gus's voice made him chuckle. Max felt confident about the casting of this odd couple. A man and a woman would be less conspicuous in the process of acquiring such a treasure. The screenplay was flawless. The actors were perfect for the roles.

Max swiveled in his chair to look at the Hollywood hills. Soon, he would be the owner of one of the rarest works of art on the planet and no one would know until it was too late to do anything about it. The most important violin in existence would soon be his. He would need to tell Jonathan about his latest escapade. Max needed to keep his right-hand man up to date. If something did go wrong, Jonathan was the ideal problem solver whose insights were invaluable.

He lit a cigar. Producer Max Pendleton arrived in Los Angeles from Chicago thirty two years ago with sixty six bucks in his pocket and an ailing 1977 Oldsmobile '88'. He came with one idea in mind: to take over the film industry. He had absolutely no knowledge of the cinema other than he liked to go to the movies. Max was twenty four years old and completely full of himself.

Within days of being in Hollywood he had bluffed his way onto the Paramount lot, convincing the security guard that he'd been mugged on Sunset Boulevard on his way to a meeting with the producers of "Happy Days". Max was a born schmoozer.

When he was eighteen years old he lied about his age to get a job as the manager of a small branch of the Ringling Brothers and Barnum and Bailey circus. The troop would be touring the mid west. Even in his teens, his burly appearance and pock-marked complexion got him into the meanest bars on the south side of Chicago. In his six months as a circus boss, there wasn't any trick in the book that he hadn't dealt with or dealt out. Max could sell Eskimos sun tan lotion.

He rotated his chair to face the small Pissarro landscape on the wall behind his desk. Standing, he moved in for a finer view of the details. If it hadn't been for Jonathan Parker's contact in Europe, he wouldn't be enjoying this up close and personal relationship with a masterpiece from the Impressionist era. It hadn't come from an auction house or been purchased from a private collection. It just arrived one day at the garden gate in a perfectly ordinary box hand-delivered by the postman.

Max tidied up his desktop then went downstairs to prepare for his wife's birthday party. He hoped that none of the staff had revealed the big surprise for the evening. It had taken a lot of pull to get Sting to pass by and serenade her with a few of her favorite songs. The Cartier necklace flown in from the shop at the Hotel de Paris in Monaco should also put a smile on her face.

Four

Maria talked to Max with her hand cupped over the mouthpiece. Gus watched the sun fading around the piazza. A shadow fell across the terrace. Their waiter was lighting candles at each table. Maria snapped the phone shut and the sound brought Gus back to earth. "It's time for a walk." She gathered up her purse and signaled for the check.

In the few minutes he'd known her, Gus realized she was used to calling the shots. He wasn't sure why Max had put them together. He decided to let it play itself out and see where it went.

Maria headed toward the basilica. Gus tagged along. After a few quick glimpses at Gus she spoke. "Tell me Mr. Gus, what do you know about the world of violins and their history?"

Gus lit a cigarette. "My grandfather had one, but I never heard him play it."

"Oh, you come from a musical family?" Maria responded enthusiastically. Gus snapped. He grabbed Maria by the arm and guided here into a dark alley. "Look," he said with his eyes on fire, "I'm a con man, a pretty damn good thief and I'm here in the middle of Italy with someone I know nothing about getting ready to knock over a museum for a violin… a violin for Christ's sake? I don't fucking believe it. I've got half a mind to chuck the whole thing and get the hell out of here pronto."

Maria made no attempt to release her arm from his grip. She stood smiling at his tirade. "My goodness, you have more of a temper than the Italians…yes?" Gus removed his hand. "I tell you Signor Gus Happy, it is as if you were going to steal a new Porsche but had never seen one. This job could set us both up for life but without the proper background on the object in question we will fail. It's as simple as that. Max hired me to be with you, to fill in the blanks but I am not working with little boys who can't take the pressure. So right now, you decide, in or out?"

Gus felt a monster headache coming on. "Okay, okay," holding his forehead, "go ahead, educate me. But I warn you, I'm not here to waste time. Max hired me to do a job, nothing more. He flicked his cigarette into a fountain. "Where do we start?"

Maria let out a maniacal giggle. "We start at my apartment where I fix us dinner. You are tired and will need much strength for our adventure."

"Our adventure" Gus thought, "What the hell is this, Harry Potter?" Right now he needed to eat and sleep. Maybe the morning would bring the picture into focus. Besides, he was too tired to argue with Sofia Loren's little sister.

Winding through the narrow streets on the other side of Strada Della Reppublica in the heart of Parma, Gus barely noticed the trendy boutiques and coffee houses dimly lit with amber or yellow lamps. Everything just swirled above and below him as if he were trying to claw his way home after an all night bender.

Maria jostled her purse for a set of keys and turned into a small courtyard overgrown with beds of flowers and guarded by an ancient olive tree.

She sprinted into the darkness to switch on the lights. Gus looked around. It felt like a smaller version of Max's mansion in

Hollywood. Educated taste permeated every nook and cranny, reeking of an indefatigable check book.

Maria threw together a pasta salad accompanied by a bottle of Chianti. Gus settled himself down on an over-sized puffy divan which begged him to fall asleep. Before he knew it they'd gone through the entire bottle of wine. Maria sat at his side with her legs in lotus position. Her empty wine glass dangled between thumb and first finger. She observed Gus for a few moments then got up and returned with a blanket and pillow. "You are too tired to work tonight. Take what I say with you to your dreams." Maria bent down to whisper in his ear. "The piece of history we are about to steal is like no other on this planet. Although there are others like it, this one is the most coveted of them all because it belonged to the Devil."

Gus heard her last words as if he were at the bottom of a well. He felt the cold pillow under his head as he sprawled out. Soon he was off the radar.

Five

Gus awoke to the sound of birds singing. He had no idea where he was. He willed his eyes to open one at a time. His left eye winced at the sudden profusion of sunlight. When he opened his right lid both eyes focused on a pair of sheer draperies fluttering in the breeze. A chill ran over him. He pulled the comforter up around his neck. A slow exaggerated yawn escaped as he pulled himself up. Through the curtains he could see Maria seated at a small table in an overgrown garden. Things looked different after a full night of sleep. Maria appeared like a goddess in her white robe, the sunlight dancing upon her face. She was calmly reading a magazine and sipping her coffee. Caffeine. Gus needed to ward off the numbness.

"Good morning!" He yelled out through a smoker's cough. With a quick snap of her head, Maria smiled and waved.

"Buon giorno" she returned, gracefully stepping in from the garden. She smiled as she scurried past him. "Stay where you are. I will bring coffee and pastries." Gus fumbled for his cigarettes, trying to shake off the coma. Maria reappeared with a tray. "You look a mess." She poured him a cup.

Gus took it and grabbed at the pastries. "What the hell time is it?"

She could barely understand him with his mouth full. "It is almost noon. I let you sleep in."

Gus drained his second cup.

Maria was in motion. "Listen, I have to dress and go shopping. We have much to do today and will not be tourists. You will find everything you need upstairs in the bathroom, first door on your right. I'll be back within the hour and we'll have a light lunch and begin your education." She let out another maniacal giggle as she went upstairs to change. Gus thought her to be the happiest woman on the face of the planet or nuts: probably both.

After she left, he decided to stroll through the apartment room by room, investigating, culling some facts about his new partner.

On the dresser in her bedroom were various framed photos of what were probably family and friends. The antique bureau was full of carefully folded lingerie and underclothes. Sexy designs which were classy but not over the top. The clothes in her closet were organized from left to right by function and color. Gus searched through all the boxes on the shelves but didn't find a weapon or any other life-threatening device. There was a spare bedroom, sparsely furnished, which didn't seem lived in.

After taking his shower he examined the medicine cabinet. It contained cold remedies and vitamins but no prescription drugs. The door was secured on a large closet in the hallway between the two rooms. He thought about picking the lock but left it alone.

Moving downstairs he headed for the kitchen. It was very modern compared to the rest of her living space. Marble counter tops, Italian appliances along with polished copper skillets which hung over the stove. The area was too neat, too perfect to be used very much. Inside the refrigerator were a tray of butter and a carton of past-use milk. She didn't appear to be a home-body.

Returning to the front room where he spent the night, he

crossed over to a small office. Inside was a huge table mounted with a computer and tower. An orange plastic box full of hard-drive discs sat next to the monitor which were numbered but not labeled. Behind the desk was a book case with subjects about art history, antiques, biographies and travel. On the top shelf rested seven books bound in black leather, untitled. Gus took one down. Scattered throughout the pages were plates of angels playing music surrounded by strange symbols and Zodiac signs. Gus returned the book carefully and stared off into space. "What makes this woman tick? Is she some kind of heavy intellectual or just out of her mind?"

Gus returned to the couch and was about to fall asleep when the rattle of the key in the front door pulled him back. He jumped up as Maria bolted in carrying three bags of groceries. He followed her into the kitchen and leaned on a counter. Maria took a quick glance at Gus. "You look much better than when I left."

Gus shuffled from one foot to the other. "You've got a great shower up there with lots of hot water. I thought hot water was a rare entity in Europe."

She continued to put things away. "Well, after they cleaned up that mess from World War II, they got real inventive and created indoor plumbing, refrigerators, central heating and many other marvelous comforts." She laughed.

"Sorry," Gus said shyly. Maria lit the top burner on the stove.

"Not a problem Signor Gus. This is your first time here. To most Americans, Europe is just full of antiquated royalty, dusty museums and people who don't take a bath every day."

He tried to make up for his remark. "Is there anything I can do to help?"

Maria was breaking eggs into a bowl. "No, just go sit at the table in the garden. I will arrive with an omelet and fresh coffee in a few minutes."

Instinctively, Gus offered Maria a military salute and headed for the back yard.

CHAPTER SIX

They ate their brunch in silence. Gus thought that the meal must have been good but his taste buds were mysteriously deadened. The extra coffee was helping, but that feeling of the unknown was hammering away inside. He placed his hands outstretched on the table.

"What now?"

"Now we begin." Maria reached over and pulled up a violin case. She opened it and removed several protective cloths. "Did you ever hold your grandfather's violin?" She handed it to Gus. It seemed really fragile. The sun sparkled across the varnish creating a liquid effect, like water racing along the shore of a shallow stream.

"Jesus Christ this thing is really light — I had no idea."

Maria countered. "Yes. The very best violins are light and delicate, whether they are fairly new like the one you are holding now, or fashioned in Cremona centuries ago."

Gus thought the violin was very old. "You'd have a hard time convincing me that this fiddle didn't have a few years behind it. This wood doesn't appear to be born yesterday. So what's the deal?

Has it been distressed like knock-off antiques with scratches, chisel marks and coffee stains?"

"Not quite," she said. "It is still possible to find wood that is centuries old from church doors and pews. If a genius maker builds a violin from these old planks even the chronologists are fooled. If the label inside looks authentic then it can sell for a small fortune and no one is the wiser." She smiled and fluffed her hair. "Okay. Somewhere in the middle of the sixteenth century the violin as we know it just 'popped out' as you Americans say. Our modern violin is almost exactly the same as it was four hundred years ago."

Gus caught her eyes before she continued. "Look," he said softly, "I quit high school in my junior year to join the family business, so please spare me the feeling that my history teacher Mrs. Watts is about to put me to sleep with an in depth discussion about the battle of Waterloo. Just tell me what I need to know."

Maria smiled at Gus. "Don't worry, I promise not to overdo it. Be patient for a few minutes."

She looked so serious and sensual at the same time. Gus smiled back. "I'm with you — shoot."

Maria downed her last dregs of coffee. "It all has to do with a small village not far from here called Cremona. A family named Amati settled there and so did Stradivari and Guarneri. These great craftsmen's violins have been more and more treasured with the centuries. Stradivari and Guarneri instruments are now priced in the millions of dollars. "

Gus interrupted. "So the violin we're supposed to get for Max is worth that kind of money?" Maria nodded back. "The one for Max is the most valuable of them all because it was played by the Devil himself. Just before he died in 1840 Niccolo Paganini donated it to the city of Genoa where it has been under lock and key ever since. It could be worth as much as ten million or more."

Gus disguised his edginess as best he could. The Devil.

Jesus, this bitch is far out. He began to think about the risk and the potential jail time if they failed. He jumped back on track. "So, tell me about this famous guy. What the hell set him apart from the others?"

"Have you ever heard the name Paganini?"

Gus shook his head.

"Okay, not everyone in the world knows this name but in the world of music he is a god. He was born in Italy in the eighteenth century and by the time he was in his twenties he had changed music forever. He was so incredible that the superstitious public thought him to be a magician or something more diabolical. Some people believed him to be in league with the Devil or possibly the Devil himself. His fingers were astonishingly fast and precise. He could imitate the sound of birds and other animals on the violin — sometimes he sounded like three or four violins playing at once. He composed his own music and for decades no one could play it but him."

Gus held up his hand. "In the States, back in the 1920's there was this black blues singer and guitarist named Robert Johnson. People believed that he met the Devil at a crossroads down south where he sold his soul in exchange for the greatest blues playing in the world."

Maria lit a cigarette. "I didn't know about that. It sounds like the same myth retold in another culture. Paganini was like a rock star today. He was tall and thin and wore his hair shoulder length. On stage he was a mysterious figure who could control his audience. He knew how to promote himself and made a lot of money."

"So this guy was the Jimi Hendrix of the violin two hundred years ago, and just like Jimi's guitars get big bucks at auction, Paganini was there first, right?"

"You've got it!" Maria said.

"So what happened to him — where did he end up?"

Maria frowned. "He became very ill in mid-life and died in

Nice, which at that time was still part of Italy. The church would not bestow last rites on his soul due to the suspicion that he was in league with the Devil. His son, Achilles, had to haul his body around for months in secret, hiding it where he could. Finally he was laid to rest in Genoa where the Devil's violin remains. The myth and legends surrounding the mysterious musician caused this instrument to be worshipped like a religious object or a precious jewel.

"Like Jimi's white Stratocaster, the one he played at Woodstock in '69." Gus said as if talking to himself.

Maria leaned over and grabbed a bottle of wine and two glasses. "History lesson over. Time for a little recess, no?" Her smile made Gus's heart beat a little faster. Maria poured while a version of 'Foxy Lady' edged its way through Gus's memory.

Seven

Giovanni Battista Sanoni locked the front door of his workshop. The windows were so mired with grime and caked with dust that very little light passed through them. The paint on the façade of his shop was peeling. It looked abandoned. He liked it that way. He needed it to be like this. His genius would remain anonymous by design.

With the aid of a pocket flashlight Giovanni returned to his work bench and turned on the lamp. Chips of wood and sawdust needed to be brushed away. All of the tools were back in their holders on the wall. He looked at his face in the mirror above the bench while replacing tops on containers of glue and varnish. "Not too bad for sixty-five years," he cooed to himself in admiration. There was hardly a blemish or wrinkle on his face. He checked the time. Soon it would be dark enough to sneak out unobserved.

He picked up his latest creation, turning it over slowly in his hands, inspecting every detail. The varnish and purfling were to perfection. Giovanni could feel the power in the wood. This copy of the Devil's violin should fool all the experts. This was his Holy Grail. Tomorrow he would string it up and have his good friend Giuseppe Como play-it-in to acquire a robust, aged sound rapidly.

A celebration was due. He reached below his bench and brought out a small bottle of Grappa. As he sipped the strong liqueur he mused over the legendary story of Paganini and J.B. Vuillaume.

One Parisian spring morning in the beginning of the nineteenth century, Niccolo Paganini arrived at the atelier of famed violin maker and inventor, J.B. Vuillaume. His precious violin had been played into exhaustion over the years and no longer sang like an angel. It needed to be restored after the countless concerts, hours of daily practice, climate changes and jostling around from bumpy coach and train rides. Wood is a living organism; when it is fatigued it sleeps.

Paganini hated to be separated from his muse of Imagination — his constant companion and confidant. Monsieur Vuillaume informed the legendary musician that at least two weeks would be required to breathe life back into the instrument. Paganini had only one option. He took it, knowing that what needed to be done would be done by a man who knew how to do it.

When he arrived two weeks later to retrieve his instrument, he was cordially greeted by J.B. Vuillaume, wearing an Arabic fez and sporting a huge smile. In each of his hands was an identical violin. Paganini went into shock. His eyes couldn't believe what he was seeing. Vuillaume allowed the game to go on for a few moments before he extended his right arm assuring Paganini that it was the original, fully restored Guarneri.

The Devil swooped up the violin while grabbing a bow from the table and started to play. As he glided over the fingerboard, bowing with intensity, his smile spread around the room. He closed his eyes in ecstasy. His heart was filled with joy. The sound of the violin roared around the shop calling workers from the benches to bathe in the maestro's pure musicianship.

After a few minutes of reconnecting with his beloved treasure, Paganini sat down in exhaustion, breathing heavily. Vuillaume asked him if the repairs were satisfactory. Paganini stood up and kissed the violin maker on both cheeks.

Ever the joker, Vuillaume offered the other violin to try out. Paganini stood back up and began to play. His eyes grew wide as the sound of the alternate instrument seemed to match, if not exceed the original. He played harder and faster and then returned to a faint pianissimo gently drawing out a slow, sanguine melody that sounded like an operatic soprano. He stopped and held the violin to his side searching Vuillaume's eyes for an explanation.

As the story goes, Vuillaume laughed as he informed the maestro that the violin he held at the moment was actually the real one. He just wanted to see if his copy could hold up to the scrutiny of the world's greatest violinist. Paganini collapsed into a chair demanding to examine both violins. The varnish on the first violin did not quite have the patina of the original. The crackling of the finish and the faded areas worn through by the sweat of the hands were not as noticeable on the copy. He bargained with Vuillaume and left the shop hurriedly with a violin under each arm.

When Paganini died, the real mystery began. The illustrious copy which had tricked the Devil himself was never seen after his death. In the past two centuries it has never been on stage, or in a private collection, or at an auction house. It just disappeared.

G.B. Sanoni switched off the lamp at his work bench and used his flashlight to get to the front door. He listened. The street was silent. He slipped out unnoticed.

CHAPTER EIGHT

Jonathan Parker sat on the sundeck of his Nichols Canyon home with a book in his lap. The sliding floor-to-ceiling glass doors of his living room were open. Strains of a Vivaldi violin concerto floated out from the stereo. Within reach was a crystal beaker filled with one hundred year old cognac. His elegant fingers fondled the raised bands of the ancient leather-bound volume.

An unforced smile of contentment that is impossible to fake spread across his face. Anyone privileged to stand near him at this moment would swear they were gazing upon a Greek god. He sipped the liqueur. A Santa Ana tossed the eucalyptus leaves back and forth within the grove which surrounded his property. He set the book down and closed his eyes against the intense sunlight. Many centuries had passed since this volume had been published against the Pope's authority in Rome. Dozens of lives had been lost over the years in the attempt to preserve its contents. How many lifetimes had he spent pouring over these arcane subjects? As he lay in the morning sun his body was reminding him of the centuries flown by. His back and knees were cramping and often painfully sore. Time was running out for his wife Emily as well.

The deck table was strewn with this morning's coffee cups and empty plates piled on top of the LA Times. Jonathan reached over and swept up the newspaper to find an article he'd read earlier. There it was. A bold statement from a scientist in Pasadena who believed he had discovered the fountain of youth through a newly patterned genetic code.

Jonathan snarled and tossed the newspaper back onto the table. He cradled the ancient book to his bosom, embracing it as if it were a dear child craving affection.

"...Fountain of youth — indeed!"

Nine

Gus tossed his travel items into a nylon bag and checked around the hotel room making sure he had everything. Basic necessities included shirts and pants, a cell phone charger and oh yes, all the separate graphite pieces of a Glock 7, ready and easy to assemble.

When he finished he thought about Maria. She was definitely a piece of work. He wasn't that experienced in handling a beautiful woman with brains. The church bells sounded from the tower of the basilica. Gus checked his watch, time to go.

Reaching for the door he stopped. He imagined his mother in the small kitchen of their Van Nuys apartment, shifting from counter to counter while fixing a meal. He never saw her smile. She must have suffocated beneath the weight of her existence with a criminal and a useless teenager. What could she have thought the day uncle Eddy came to take her son for a ride? Gus pictured her face as they drove away. It was as if she were watching a bus load of strangers.

As the Alpha whisked through the Tuscan countryside not a word was exchanged. Maria focused on her driving while Gus nodded off. A sharp turn on the mountain road jarred him back to consciousness. He shuffled in his bucket seat. "So, are we picking up a violin in Cremona or just doing more homework?"

Maria down shifted. "We're checking with Signor Sanoni."

Gus jumped in. "…Signor who? What the hell is this all about?"

Maria pulled off to the shoulder. She removed her sunglasses and looked into Gus's eyes.

"When you arrived in Parma three days ago, you thought you were being followed."

"Yeah, you were following me."

Maria stared down at the steering wheel. "I was following the man who was following you, not you."

Gus fished nervously for a cigarette. "Huh? No one knows I'm here but you and Max."

"I would like to believe that, my friend, but now I'm not sure." Maria became pensive. "Someone aware of your presence for any reason does complicate things. We must, as you Americans say, 'lay back' and observe for awhile." As her words trailed off she began to scan the surrounding hilltops as if she were searching for a sniper in the woods.

"You haven't answered my question." Gus said impatiently. "Who is this Sanoni character and what does he have to do with the job?"

Maria started the engine, letting it idle. "Signor Sanoni is one of the best violin forgers in the world, maybe the best. We are going to Cremona to pick up the copy of the Devil's violin Max commissioned. The plan is to exchange it for the real one in the museum in Genoa within two weeks."

Gus was losing it. "Damn decent of you to share the plan with me. I don't work in the dark. Information from A to Z is the only option; it's basic to keeping my ass out of trouble."

Maria tossed Gus's hair. "Easy Gus, you're acting the little boy again. But you're right. I should have told you the whole plan. I was just waiting — waiting to get to know you better to see if…"

"To see if I could be trusted? To see if I was fucking smart enough to keep up with your wicked ass?" The veins in his neck were popping out. "Believe me honey, now that I know what the goal is, I could handle it all by myself. Knock over an old museum in Italy for one fucking fiddle? No problem!"

Maria grabbed the steering wheel tightly as she stared ahead. Gus thought that his blood pressure was going through the roof and just wanted to calm down long enough to sort through the bullshit in front of him.

Maria relaxed her grip. "I too spend my time observing people. I like you Gus. I admire the way you went through my apartment without going too far. You showed me a lot of class." Gus shot a sideways glance at Maria. "And besides," she continued, "I would have thought less of you if you hadn't checked me out. I know more about you than you think."

Gus lit another cigarette without offering her one. "Like what?"

"How about the twenty dollar U.S. government plates you smuggled out of Mexico in 1998, for starters?"

Gus recoiled. "How in the hell…?"

Maria cut him off. "It doesn't matter, but you see, I am very thorough and my connections are extremely reliable."

Gus kept looking into her face trying to find answers to questions he wasn't sure he could even formulate. The only other person who knew about the Mexico job was a dead Mafioso in Vegas. He knew he was in deep waters. Now he needed to fish his way out. "Okay, so what's this vacation thing all about?"

Maria gunned the engine and put the car into first gear. "The vacation is a precautionary move to see if I'm right about someone following you." She took a glance into the rear view mirror. "If they are, then they will certainly not be far behind us. Maybe I'm imagining things. We'll just have to play a little game of wait and see." Maria let out the clutch and shot onto the road leaving a cloud of dust behind them.

A man dressed in black had pulled his rent-a-car off the road a kilometer behind Gus and Maria. He replaced the electronic listening device into his black briefcase. He watched them pull away as he lit a gold-tipped cigarillo. She's a sharp one, he reflected. He smoked casually and when he finished, pulled onto the road heading for Cremona at a very relaxed pace.

Ten

Giuseppe Como let out a half-muffled groan as early afternoon sunlight invaded his small apartment off of via Stradivari. He was not ready to face the day. Valerie's perfume permeated the stillness of the room. He stroked the crater in the pillow left by her head full of golden hair. She was perfect. Never in his uneven life had he known someone so beautiful and so insightful. Most people did not understand the relationship between a musician and their instrument, particularly a violinist and their violin. Valerie did.

Giuseppe stared up at the ceiling, counting the candles in the chandelier. It was his usual waking routine. There were only ten, but every day he counted them several times before getting up. He rolled over to his right and touched the handle of his violin case under the bed. He didn't need to play it right now; he just needed to know that it was there.

From the time that Giuseppe was a child he heard his father playing the violin. The music crackled across the tiled floor of the family villa in Rome. A strange occurrence happened just before his sixth birthday. His father played as usual but Giuseppe heard the sound in a different way. It was as if he were inside the instrument. By some fairy-tale magic, the pureness of the violin's voice captivated him. From that day on the violin became a mysterious friend and teacher: his constant companion.

Right now, he desperately needed a coffee. He had an appointment at four o'clock with Signor Sanoni to play a new violin. Giuseppe adored the violin maker for his eccentric ways. There was always the whispered phone call with a time and a meeting place as if the two of them were planning to overthrow a government or steal plans for a rocket. It always made Giuseppe laugh but at the same time, he knew what a genius the man was. And besides, there was the money. He was paid handsomely for the pure pleasure of breathing life into these new icons of music.

Suddenly Giuseppe's heart raced. He heard footsteps in the hallway. It must be Valerie returning with pastries or to make him some coffee. The door creaked open and to Giuseppe's surprise, there stood a man completely dressed in black, smoking a gold-tipped cigarillo, with a smile that made the hairs on the back of Giuseppe's neck stand up.

Eleven

Gus was confused. After checking into a hotel on the outskirts of Cremona, Maria answered her cell phone with an exuberant smile which quickly disappeared. Listening to the caller in abject silence, she seemed to be imploding. Her shoulders shriveled up as she hunched over the phone rocking back and forth on the edge of the bed.

The sign on the hotel room door said 'no smoking' in four languages. Gus lit up, feeling something was really wrong. When Maria finished the call she sat in place as if she were alone. Gus tried to keep it light. "So what's the matter, couldn't get the dinner reservations you were counting on?"

Without looking up she replied, "We are, as you Americans say, in deep shit. That was Signor Sanoni. He just found his partner Giuseppe Como with his throat slit. He's dead." Tears were trickling down her cheeks.

Gus put his hand on her shoulder. "His partner...I don't understand, I thought you told me he worked alone in secret?"

Maria waved him away as if he were a small child with a

stupid question. "He does work alone. Giuseppe was a violinist who broke in the new instruments so they would sound old very quickly. If you're going to fool a buyer the instrument must not only look aged but sound that way also." She stared off into space.

Gus thought that their two bed hotel room with nothing on the walls resembled a sparse jail cell. He pulled up a chair and sat facing Maria. "Okay," he began, "somebody slit the kid's throat — what has that got to do with us? Maybe it was something personal? You know, a friend or lover out of control, even a robbery. Did the kid have a violin with him? Maybe someone wanted to snatch it and he got in the way?"

Maria cut him off. "Sanoni's contact at the police told him there was no robbery. Everything was in place. The violin was in the case. His wallet, money, watch, ring and cell phone — nothing missing."

Gus thought it over for a few moments and lit another cigarette. "I guess this is going to cut short our vacation, right?"

Maria sighed. "Not funny! Giuseppe was my friend. I'm wondering now about the person I saw following you. Does he know our plan?"

Gus jumped in. "I can tell by your look that something is running around in that brain of yours that you have not quite figured out how to tell me. There must be a much bigger picture that I haven't been shown yet." Gus stood up. "God damn it, every time I work for Max there's something under the table waiting to yank my Johnson."

Maria flashed a startled look. "I need to know right now what this heist is really about. Are we doing the old violin switcheroo or am I about to have some CIA or FBI weenie up my ass?"

Gus stopped as Maria's cell phone went off like a three alarm fire. She sat still listening. Gus reached inside his jacket pocket for another cigarette but the pack was empty. He crumpled it up and tossed it across the room, missing the trash can by a mile.

Maria closed her cell and jumped up. Without looking at

Gus she said, "We have to leave right now. We must meet Signor Sanoni in a forest south of here to pick up the violin."

Gus waved his arms in front of her. "Whoa…hold on a minute. We're going nowhere until you fill me in on the big picture."

She knew her back was against the wall. "My years of research have led me to believe that there may also be a set of documents hidden in the lining of the Devil's violin case. The museum must still have it. It is a piece of history just like the violin."

"Documents — research? What is this, a school project?"

Maria lay back on the bed and stared at the ceiling. "Paganini was also a member of a secret society which was very powerful in his day. The membership was dedicated to Universal Reformation, to bring about equality throughout the world: religious tolerance and so much more."

"More?" Gus stammered. "What, some kind of Free Masonic garbage full of super human powers and funny handshakes? Bull shit! We go for the fiddle and that's it…understand?"

Maria offered an unconvincing nod. Gus went into the bathroom to get his shaving kit. When he returned, Maria was still on the bed with that only-a-woman-knows-how-to look of sensuality that begs forgiveness.

Gus briefly contemplated her and headed for the door.

CHAPTER TWELVE

Twelve

Special FBI Agent Chris Clarke was a very simple man with a straight-ahead view of life. He did not own an iPod, preferring the roar of the wind upon the waves when he strolled along the beach. Life on the streets was hectic. The need for periods of peace and quiet was a necessity. While studying art history and restoration at college, his professors thought him to be a natural — one who can sense a fake through intuition. Chris spent many off days in museums enjoying the beauty and silence.

The medals of valor he collected during his stint in Desert Storm displayed his special forces training. This combination of introspection coupled with the capacity to wreak physical havoc was the touchstone of his success. His salt and pepper personality allowed him to confront his own demons and deal with those on the streets.

His career began with the perfect family: his wife Brenda and their two children, Chris junior and Sarah. Only one problem: In the late nineties Chris and his crew were trying to find a two year old girl kidnapped in Alabama. FBI photos of the child reminded

Chris of his daughter Sarah. The Bureau got close to apprehending the kidnapper but he managed to stay one frustrating step ahead. On the final day of the showdown, detective Clarke arrived at the location in Huntsville five minutes too late. The victim lay on a small cot covered in her own blood, while the murderer sat hunched up in a corner of the cabin laughing. Chris was ready to tear the perpetrator's heart out. Fortunately, his colleagues restrained him. That day, something inside Christopher Patrick Clarke snapped.

After returning to the FBI base of operations in Los Angeles for a debriefing, he headed home. But he first made a quick stop at Ray's Liquor on Pico Boulevard to pick up a bottle of vodka. After tucking the kids into bed he sat up all night and polished off most of the bottle. This routine went on for two months and finally Brenda called the Bureau to seek help. The administration engaged an in-house psychologist to interview Chris.

Dr. Miriam Watkins began to counsel Chris. The sessions went all too well. Doctor and patient found an immediate attraction for each other and within three sessions they were into it. You can guess the rest. Brenda found out and filed for a divorce. She packed up the kids and moved to Boulder, Colorado to be near her sister. The day they left, Chris watched them drive away. Chris junior and Sarah stared out the back window looking like two street urchins in a Dickens novel. In the meantime, the ever neurotic Miriam Watkins decided that she was still in love with her lesbian partner of five years and dumped Chris.

Chris never had time to feel sorry for himself. He was transferred to the San Diego Bureau, where he bought a small condo in South Mission Beach. His life was back on track. All of his recent assignments had been successfully closed. He hadn't touched alcohol for over two years and quit smoking a year ago.

Monday morning he headed for the Bureau in downtown San Diego, as usual. He loved to start his week this way, top down on his 1972 Porsche 911, sporting a big smile behind his air force sunglasses. Chris Clarke never failed to appreciate where he lived and how his luck had held out. That was until today. A heavy rain began halfway to the office. Not a good omen.

Thirteen

Alistair checked his gold Rolex. Milan was only thirty minutes away. He loved to drive in Europe. It wasn't the same as the U.S. There were never any police or Highway patrol cars hugging your rear bumper. He had hesitated leaving his home in Savannah, Georgia for Italy so quickly after his last episode in Europe, but it couldn't be helped. It was a matter of honor. Now was the time to gather the family history and most importantly, to possess the treasure his thrice-great grandfather had left behind.

His informants on the west coast had tipped him to the fact that a big shot in California had begun to initiate a plan to steal the violin that Alistair believed should be his. He was the last in the family line. He would merely follow the thieves and collect the item at the end of the process.

Alistair was not a social animal. He didn't have any friends — just clients who wouldn't know his name and never saw him. Secrecy was the key to success for a seasoned professional of the highest standards.

After checking into the four star Royal Garden Hotel in

Milan he was on his way to Leonardo Maggio's fashions for men. While selecting sport jackets, Alistair thought about the incident in Cremona. Would it stop the competition in their tracks? They were a cute couple. He'd like to get to know them better. But of course, if they just somehow disappeared…that would be fine.

The valet opened the lobby door. A young bellman quickly arrived to take charge of the shopping bags. Alistair flicked his gold-tipped cigarillo into the street, smiling at the opulence awaiting him as he passed over the threshold.

Fourteen

Some people are just born to be big. The son of a Mexican father and an American mother, both over six feet in height, Carlos Portman Gonzales grew at an alarming rate. By the time he was sixteen he was nearly as tall as his parents and weighed two hundred pounds, nearly all muscle. He didn't just play on the football team in school, he *was* the football team.

His first day in high school marked his destiny. A tough kid from Boston named Frank had just arrived on the scene and wanted to establish himself as the main-man. He chose Carlos as his first punching bag. Big mistake. Frank confronted the gentle giant at the student lockers and cussed him out. Carlos listened patiently to his tirade then shrugged his shoulders and headed for sociology, leaving Frank mad as hell.

Carlos Gonzales had a passion for food that quickly earned him the nick name "Chubbs" from his class mates. That same day, Frank came up with a plan. He would catch Chubbs off guard at lunch time and beat the shit out of him in front of the entire student body.

While Chubbs was cruising through sandwich number three for his afternoon energy break, Frank attacked him from behind. Another big mistake. With Frank's arms securely wound around Chubb's massive neck, the mild-mannered Latino casually stood up and carried the surprised attacker effortlessly to the nearest trash bin where he dumped him along with his left over lunch bag in the same motion. Then he closed the lid and locked it. The shell-shocked tough guy could be heard pounding and screaming his way deeper into the garbage. That was the first and last time anyone in the next four years of high school ever approached Chubbs Gonzales with anything but a smile on their face.

To the advantage of this massively strong individual, he was also sensitive, with an IQ that matched his physical size. Way off the charts. He was equipped to do anything he chose with his life. He had only one dream: to be the best agent of Latino heritage to ever make the ranks of the FBI.

Fifteen

Chris Clarke's mind was drifting. Maybe it was just a Monday morning thing. Maybe it was his dinner date that was canceled just before he was to pick her up. Since closing his last case involving a ring of passport forgers he didn't have anything on the books to grab his attention.

As a teenager, Chris had read all of Arthur Conan Doyle's magical stories about the infamous Sherlock Holmes. Even at that age, Chris related to the great detective's bouts with boredom.

Chris sat in his office. He swiveled lazily with his back to the door, looking out at the people bustling around Horton Plaza, four floors below. The fountain in the center of the plaza was hypnotic, shooting its geyser into the slight breeze coming from the bay two blocks away.

Suddenly he felt a presence and turned around. The massive figure of Chubbs Gonzales filled the entire doorway. His feet were spread apart with his muscle-packed arms folded in front of him.

"Okay, so who am I?"

Chris looked him up and down. "Hell, I don't know. You could be a Mexican with a glandular problem or maybe the first Chicano wrestler in an Armani suit to make it across the border?"

Chubbs entered the office and sat down. "That was stupid of me boss, I was just trying to break it to you gently."

For a brief moment their eyes made crazy-glue contact. "Okay, lay it on me."

Chubbs shifted in the chair too small for his body. "I thought you'd guess it right off the top."

"Well I didn't, Mr. Charades, so perhaps you could enlighten me now?"

"You know," Chubbs ambled slightly, "Men in Black, or more precisely, 'the man in black — the Bureau thinks he's back."

Chris froze. Five years ago he had assisted Parisian law enforcement in tracking down the thieves of a rare seventeenth century statuette stolen from a private collection. He was asked to stay on to assist in what turned out to be a failed pursuit of the contract killer known throughout Europe as the "man in black." This assignment remained the only unsolved case in Chris's career. The origin of the hired assassin was unknown. No fingerprints, DNA, hair, or clothing fibers had ever been found at a crime scene other than the victims'. Witnesses had only glimpsed a man dressed totally in black, before and after the murders, who seemed to vanish into thin air.

Less than a year later, a United States Senator from Texas was found in his home outside of Dallas with his throat cut from ear to ear. Neighbors had seen a man dressed totally in black leaving the premises after the assault. The FBI initiated a total commitment to apprehend this assassin and a co-operation pact was signed between the FBI and Interpol, which gave the FBI co-op jurisdiction in Europe as long as proper notification was arranged before any investigation was begun.

What Agent Clarke and the department knew for sure was that the "man in black" was a killer for hire with no apparent political ties, who was capable of getting close enough to his victims to cut their throats with surgical precision.

Chris finished his mental review. "So what's got the Bureau thinking our 'man' is back on the scene?"

Chubbs pulled out a BlackBerry. "Okay, we have a murder victim, one, Giuseppe Como, of Italian nationality, found with his throat cut in his own bed. Location is Cremona, Italy."

Chris broke in. "What's our man doing now, trying to wipe out the world's population of violinists?"

Startled, Chubbs countered, "How in the heck did you know he was a violinist?"

"Jesus, I didn't. I thought everyone knew that in Cremona people either build the damn things or play them."

Chubbs looked up briefly from the illuminated screen. "Uh huh….continuing along here, the body was discovered by his friend, a violin repairman named Giovanni Sanoni. They had an appointment that afternoon that the fiddler missed. Sanoni went around to his apartment to find him, then he called the police when there was no answer on his phone or at the door."

Slightly impatient, Chris asked, "We got any info on this Sanoni character?"

"Already been there, ran him through the Global computer — he's clean. Not even a traffic violation: sixty-five year old Italian, born in Parma, residing in Cremona for the past twenty years. Something a little odd though. Italian authorities have no records of his existence prior to his arrival in Cremona. Between his birth and the next forty-five years we seem to have a little gap."

Chris felt Excedrin headache number fifty coming on. "Okay, now tell me how we connect the dots and put our *'homme en noir'* in the middle of this crime?"

Chubbs looked up with a furrowed brow, "Our…what?"

Chris scowled. "It's French for man in black. Didn't you study any foreign languages before you graduated at the top of your class from UCLA?"

"Oh, sure, Taiwanese," Chubbs asserted, "Just enough to order from the menu at the Thai Princess on Beverly Boulevard." Chris frowned. Chubbs continued. "Anyway, the MO is the same. Surgical cut, and witnesses who saw a man dressed from head to toe in black entering and leaving the premises. We have a total of three witnesses. A mother and daughter who were on their balcony trying to stay cool and a business man in his apartment with the door open. It was over a hundred that day."

"Hmm…if it is our *man*, he's taken a contract that doesn't appear to have the usual focus. Most of his victims in the past have had political connections at a very high level. We'd better do a background search on our fiddler to see if we can find a connection. Maybe he doubled as a spy?"

Chubbs responded. "I ran him through Global also. Everything comes up a big fat zero,"

Chris's intuition was kicking in. He could feel something big was in the offing. Why would a violinist be murdered for no apparent reason? What was the appointment about concerning Sanoni and Como? Why were there no records on Sanoni prior to his arrival in Cremona?"

Chris was aware that the violin world was a mysterious place. His neighbor in San Diego was a violinist with the symphony. He knew many tales of intrigue, fraud and deception which permeated the acquisition of a fine violin and its related instruments.

Would someone go so far as murder to own one of these icons? Had someone done that now? Was there a rare violin involved here that had not surfaced yet?

Chris wrapped up his meeting with Chubbs and signed out for lunch. He headed to the Fire Station, his favorite burger eatery in Mission Beach. Taking in the view of the ocean from the second floor terrace, FBI special Agent Chris Clarke wondered what the weather was like in Italy.

Sixteen

Early morning sunlight invaded Gus's eyes again as he awoke on Maria's sumptuous white couch with another kink in his back. It was day five after his arrival. The sun was full bore but his head was full of clouds. What had just happened? How did a relatively text-book swap and run turn into such a nightmare? Maria had hardly said three words since they returned from Cremona. The murder of Giuseppe Como had cast a dark shadow on their temporary partnership.

He lit a cigarette and began thinking. When they met Signor Sanoni in the forest to pick up the copy of the violin, something strange had occurred that Gus was just now filtering through his brain. Maria and Signor Sanoni had stood very close to each other and talked way too long for two people who shouldn't be seen together after the murder of their mutual friend. They then exchanged small packages and a goodbye kiss. What was their relationship?

Gus sped around the apartment in his boxer shorts looking for Maria. She was gone. He checked her parking spot. The Alpha was not there. He dressed and headed into the den. The doors were closed when he went to sleep. This morning they were open. A good thief remembers the order of things in a room he burgles. After shuffling things around to find the prize, returning everything to its original location was an important trick to stall the victims before they realized a crime had been committed.

He slowly scanned the space trying to remember things as they were days before. The computer screen and the keyboard seemed untouched. He felt the tower, it was not warm. He flipped open the box of hard-discs. They were all there. Next, he took a brief inventory of the furniture. Everything seemed to be as he remembered except that a chair that had been near the desk was now over by the window. Gus approached the chair thinking that the new location would be ideal for reading a book by sunlight. That thought turned his attention to the book case. He stood in front of the library for two minutes trying to figure out what was different. The ancient books on the top shelf were six instead of seven. Maria must have taken one of the volumes with her this morning. Only one question remained: what in the hell is going on?

Gus knew one thing for sure. It was time to assemble his Glock and have it ready at a moment's notice.

Seventeen

Jonathan Parker sat facing Max Pendleton's desk. The top floor of Pendleton's mansion had always been one of Jonathan's favorite spots. A sense of serenity came over him. Max shuffled papers. Jonathan had no idea why he was summoned.

"We've got a problem." Max was never one to waste words.

Jonathan probed. "Surely not concerning the currency exchange we concluded last week. We made a bundle."

Max adjusted his two hundred and forty pound bulk. "No, it's not that. You did a beautiful job as usual and as you say, we made a bundle. It's something else. I think you're the only person on the face of the earth that could understand." Max switched off his computer, removed his glasses and rubbed his eyes. "You see, I hated like hell to sell that eighteenth century Del Gesu last week, but it was necessary for future business in the Middle East. That sector is opening up to cinema, big time!"

"I understand," Jonathan replied with the mixed tone of a priest and an attorney.

Max looked at Jonathan with a mischievous smile. "Why in

the hell do you think I hired you?" Jonathan shrugged. "I found out about your Wall Street investment skills after I heard your concert at the church in Beverly Hills."

Jonathan sat straighter. He'd almost forgotten about his solo violin concert a decade ago.

Max pulled out two Havana cigars, lit one and passed the other to Jonathan. "You see," Max puffed vigorously, "When I was a kid running the circus, there was a family troupe that did a trapeze act that was a big draw. They had a daughter named Giselle that I fell in love with. One day while inspecting the grounds I heard the most gorgeous music, as if an angel were singing. I followed the sound and found Giselle playing the violin. I froze. She turned and saw me and looked scared, as if she had done something wrong. I rushed towards her and threw my arms around her. She damn near dropped the fiddle. I held her in my arms. She didn't resist." Max paused to examine his cigar and stared at the ceiling. "For the next two weeks the family kept to themselves and one day they just disappeared after a Saturday matinee. I was devastated. I couldn't go on with the circus. I gave notice and went back to Chicago."

Jonathan fondled his cigar then returned it to the desk. He hadn't lit it yet. Max interpreted this as a sign of boredom. "Are you following me on this one or not?"

Jonathan quickly fixed his piercing eyes on Max's. "You'll have to pardon me, I was listening to every word you said and it is of course an interesting piece of your history. But at the same time I was asking myself a question."

"And that would be?" Max returned.

Jonathan cut the tip off of the cigar. "Well," Jonathan lit his cigar, "I was just wondering who in the world could have made that violin you passed off as a Guarneri last week. It was really excellent and had me fooled for a few minutes."

Max was shocked. "What in the hell are you getting at, Jonathan?"

Jonathan exhaled the smoke slowly. "Look Max, you and I have conducted business for a long time with no deception between us. The other five violins in your case were genuine. The one you sold to Ahmed was a copy, a damn good one. So my curiosity is uncontrollable. I can only think of three craftsmen in the world who could pull it off: two in America and one in Europe."

With a big smile, Max cut in. "You forgot Sanchez in Argentina."

Jonathan replied calmly. "No I didn't. His varnishes have never been good enough to fool that many experts."

Max burst out laughing. "Jesus Christ, Jonathan, you take the fucking cake! I've never known anyone like you and may never again as long as I live."

Jonathan set his cigar in the ash tray. "Now perhaps we could discuss why you requested my presence here this morning?"

 Eighteen

A fly buzzed lazily around Maria's face. She made an unconscious attempt to shoo it away, but it kept returning and she gave up. It was difficult to focus after the tragic event of yesterday.

Giuseppe Como was someone she admired. He commanded great skill and power over the violin yet never showed off. His sound was the soul of his talent. He played to serve music, not the other way around. Giuseppe was everything that she wanted to be as a musician when she began to study the violin. Tears formed on the brink of falling but she held them back. Twenty five years ago she lived a blissful life practicing countless hours with little effort because she loved it so. As a child, the violin was her whole world. Yet, like so many young persons who begin a journey dedicated to music, with all of the enthusiasm and self-confidence to go along with it, fate had other plans.

In her early twenties Maria had a chance meeting in Paris with an American violinist named Jonathan Parker. She attended his concert and went back stage to meet him afterwards. Although he did not teach officially, he accepted her as a student.

Lessons with Jonathan Parker consisted of listening to him play. He would close his eyes and draw the bow slowly across the strings creating a heavenly sound of beauty. When he stopped, he would smile as if returning from another world. One day when Maria arrived for her lesson at his hotel, the concierge informed her that Mr. Parker had departed for the United States and that he had left her a package.

The envelope contained a small book printed in London in 1888. It was a story about an Indian princess from antiquity whose beauty was unmatched. Her one desire as a child was to play an instrument called the Tanpura. It was an integral part of classical music from the Orient. Her father, the Sultan, forbade her to waste her time with such nonsense, so to spite him, she ran away with a handsome vagabond who was the most daring thief in India. Together, they amassed a fortune in precious stones. The couple built a house along the bank of a holy river and gave most of their rubies and emeralds to the poor. With some of the booty that they kept, the princess acquired the most beautiful Tanpura in all of India. They were never caught and lived happily the rest of their lives with her music accompanying the bright jewels in the sky at night.

After Jonathan left Paris, Maria read the story over and over, wondering what it meant?

One night while clubbing in Parma she met the infamous antique dealer Raphael Costella. He had a reputation that was world-wide in certain circles. His knowledge of antiques was unrivaled: his propensity to deal in quality copies and turn them over as the original article was also well known. His "fakes" occupied space in elite mansions throughout Europe and the United States.

Raphael offered Maria a job and soon she became his assistant. Over time he tutored her in the sly practices of deceptive antique dealing. She became a crafty and cultured thief: the parable of the Indian princess was Jonathan's prediction about her future.

Jonathan had somehow foreseen the direction her life would take. Or, she thought, had he made it happen? Maria had always been aware of an unearthly quality about Jonathan Parker. She remembered how many of her lessons seemed as if she had stepped into a dream, suddenly evaporating when the lesson ended.

Maria began to pack for the trip to the family cabin in the mountains south of Borgotaro. It was up to her to play-in G.B. Sanoni's copy of the Devil's violin. She had not been practicing for months. It would take a few days to limber up her fingers and bow arm. She thought about Gus. How would they get along in the mountains for two weeks? What about the stranger that haunted their lives? Was he following them? Did he murder Giuseppe?

Maria closed her suitcase and took out the violin holding it up to the light to admire its beauty. She strummed the open strings with her thumb. She smiled.

CHAPTER NINETEEN

Nineteen

The classic 1964 ivory white Mercedes 300se eased its way into the driveway shutting down in front of the garage. The driver remained motionless. He was mulling over the events that had taken place on this calm Saturday morning in Hollywood. The sun roof was drawn back and he stared at the myriad of pine tree branches, eucalyptus and maple leaves dancing in the breeze. After a few minutes Jonathan Parker exited the car to find Emily waiting for him at the front door.

"So, how was your meeting with Max?" She offered her husband a sincere kiss on the cheek.

"Interesting to say the least," he replied as he tucked her under his right arm. Once inside, he poured himself a malt whisky and settled into his favorite chair. "I've always known about the maniacal side of Max's passion for antiques, but this morning I think he's really out done himself."

Emily's eyes widened with interest. "What does he want to do now, hang the Mona Lisa on his bedroom wall?"

"Not far from it," Jonathan chortled, "the bloody fool wants to own the world's most prized violin, Paganini's Guarneri, which has been housed in the museum in Genoa for a century and a half." He sipped his whisky. "Maria and Gus Happy have been paired up to steal it and are leading the charge in Italy as we speak."

"Surely you must be joking?" Emily responded.

"I only wish I were." Jonathan rubbed the back of his neck. "What concerns me is that Max put this in motion without consulting me first. His plan is not badly thought out, but bringing me on board after the start does limit my influence and I don't like that at all."

Emily whispered. "But dear, how does this concern us?"

Jonathan reached for her hand. "Let's retire to the vault and I'll explain."

The stillness inside their Nichol's Canyon home was only interrupted by the steady ticking of an ancient grandfather clock which had been in Jonathan's family's possession for over two centuries. Inside their secret chamber accessible through a sliding panel next to the fireplace, the Parkers sat quietly at a seventeenth-century table. The legs were painted with black roses and carved with figures of gargoyles. A massive red candle in the center of the table was the only source of illumination. The walls were lined with hand–written manuscripts dating back centuries alongside leather-bound books decorated with occult symbols.

Jonathan spoke after a meditative silence. "I've never told you about the documents in Paganini's possession at the time of his death."

Emily stared into the candle's flame. "You did tell me years ago that Paganini claimed to have possessed a method which would reveal the secrets of his technique. Are these papers related?"

Jonathan sighed. "It's much more than that my dear. This set of documents, if indeed they still exist, would be indispensible to both of us: to our future, to our very existence."

Emily listened carefully to the sound of her husband's timeless voice resonating off the walls of their sanctum sanctorum, mixed with the flickering hiss of the candle's wick. She knew that Jonathan was devoted to Maria and had mentored her in Paris. Max had involved her in his latest scheme and Emily knew they would need to watch over her; to protect her if necessary.

She didn't need to discuss her own physical decline with her husband. Their silence upon the subject said everything. If the alchemical formula which Paganini inserted in the violin case housing the real Devil's violin would aid them in their attempt to extend their lifespan, then they must leave for Europe immediately.

One thing was for sure: more than one life was at stake.

CHAPTER TWENTY

Gus sat down on the porch of Maria's mountain cabin. The air was much thinner at this altitude and he drew it slowly into his lungs while his eyes scanned the landscape for any signs of movement. On top of the table was his bag and a chipped porcelain coffee cup full of strong brew. He brought his hands together in a powerful clap. The sound reverberated back at him three times. The front of the cabin was less than fifty yards from a small stream backed by sheer granite cliffs. The narrow dirt road that led from the main highway was the only way in or out. The rear of the cabin was surrounded by a massive pine forest so thick with branches and foliage that barely any light filtered through. It would be damn hard for anyone to sneak up on them. Any vehicle approaching from as far off as a half a mile could be heard.

Maria moved around inside the cabin, organizing. She kept glimpsing over at the violin case. She was waiting for it to call her over — to commence the dance.

Gus rummaged around inside his bag searching for the

folder of paper work and photos which Maria downloaded. He pulled out a carton of Camels, took out a fresh pack and lit up. He placed the folder on the table. He heard the snaps of the violin case followed shortly by Maria tuning up. He began to wonder if he could put up with two weeks of violin, no matter how beautiful it sounded.

The first item out of the folder was a Google satellite view of the museum that housed the Devil's violin. The photo had been zoomed in to expose the building and the surrounding streets for four blocks in all directions. The second shot was closer, offering more detail of the roof and the immediate streets on all sides. The final four pictures were from the Genoa chamber of commerce site. Gus silently thanked the persons who were thoughtful enough to include so many detailed shots of the interior as well as the exterior of the museum.

Gus finished his coffee and lit another cigarette. He was sure now that they would need to visit the location before attempting the swap. "Christ," Gus thought, "I don't even know where in the hell Genoa is or how long it takes to get there."

Gus heard Maria draw the bow over the open strings, one at a time, spending several seconds on each string. She paused for a moment and then repeated the process. This time the second string sounded scratchy. Gus heard her curse, "*Managgia la Madonna!*"

"Oh boy," he thought, "the fun is just beginning."

Twenty-One

It was now eight in the evening and the view from Chris Clarke's FBI Bureau window onto the Horton plaza below resembled a ghost town. The extreme August heat had emptied downtown San Diego. The historic fountain in the middle of the plaza was abandoned.

Chris had just finished a non-stop marathon of paper work. Updated files on the "man in black," as well as the murder victim Giuseppe Como and his friend G.B. Sanoni were scattered around his desk. Some questions were answered and some were still hanging out in the ether as usual in circumstances such as these.

He still had no idea what he was actually dealing with. The only reason the FBI took an interest in the murder of the violinist was the possibility that the "man in black" may have been involved. The big question looming around the Bureau was motive. Up to this point the contract killings attributed to this assassin had been political figures. There was no reason to suspect that the newest victim had political ties.

Chris Clarke liked facts. He had discovered that G.B. Sanoni drew out large sums of cash, anywhere from one to three thousand Euros at a crack, five or six times a year which closely matched deposits made by Giuseppe Como, one to three days later.

Another curious piece of information was the fact that out of over 150 separately operated violin shops in Cremona, not one was under the name G.B. Sanoni. He was just a repairman for a maker named Marcel Wittenberg of Bavaria. Through the Violin Makers Association of Europe web site, there was no trace of a violin in the marketplace with a label from G.B. Sanoni. If G.B. Sanoni did not fashion violins, but was just a repairman, what could have been the relationship between him and the murdered violinist that involved thousands of Euros?

Chris paused to take a sip of his room temperature Starbucks double espresso. He didn't notice the bitter taste. He was deep into his unique thought process that took over on every case. A mental state of intuitive analysis arrived after a period of fact gathering. He sat with his eyes closed for a few minutes and then it happened.

He bolted upright in his chair. "That's it!" He shouted to an empty room. "Sanoni must have a secret workshop where he makes copies of the great masters. That's why there are no violins attributed to him. He hired Como to break them in."

Chris set aside his revelation for a moment to re-read a report from the Mayor's office in Parma referring to a catastrophic event. One piece of the mysterious puzzle surrounding G.B. Sanoni could now be put to rest. Twenty years ago there had been a fire in the county records building in Parma which destroyed birth certificates and criminal records kept in paper files and index cards. Along with thousands of others, G.B. Sanoni had been the victim of a complete erasure of his life history. His first forty-five years did not exist.

Special FBI Agent Chris Clarke was getting that old feeling again. A cold shiver traveled along his spine. His instinct was undeniable. If there is no political connection to this case then it has to be related to the violin world. Some plan of a major theft must be under way. Was the "man in black" in the picture? Chris would need to go to Italy and talk with G.B. Sanoni and sniff out the details.

He glanced at the clock. It was past nine o'clock. It was time to call it a day and head out for Red's Barbecue on Mission boulevard.

Chris was just taking his first bite of ribs when his cell phone went off.

"Hey boss man," Chubbs Gonzales screamed into Chris's ear, "wha's up?"

Chris, with a mouthful said, "Yo, beaner-breath, get your passport out, we're heading for Europe in a couple of days. It's time for your ass to taste something other than tacos and Thai food."

Chris could feel Chubb's ear-to-ear grin over the air waves.

CHAPTER TWENTY-TWO

Twenty-Two

Every morning began in the same way for the thirty seven year old woman whose last name is a man's first name. Her red eyes popped open around five a.m. and she blinked several times while sitting up in lotus position accompanied by the eerie fluorescent glow of her digital clock. It didn't matter when she went to sleep; her inner alarm kicked in before dawn each day.

She sought help from a psychologist. After several tests it was concluded that her problem was stress related to her occupation — female FBI agent, field-active and dispensed around the globe where needed.

Ariel George was raised by her father. She thought about him every morning in the cold darkness of her apartment on Beacon Hill in Boston or in whatever hotel room in whichever state or country she had been assigned. She was her own role model but had inherited his discipline. Ariel was devoted to her career and her fellow agents.

Two months ago, for the first time in her fifteen years with the FBI she had drawn her service weapon and saved a fellow agent's life by downing the perpetrator before he discharged his firearm. She had killed a suspect in the line of duty. She was deemed a hero and had saved a colleague's life. But, it was not the practice range. Good guy, bad guy, she had taken a life, and the incident was haunting her dreams. This was a sign of weakness she would have to deal with on her own.

Being raised by a single male parent had shaped her life. She was the neighborhood tom-boy. She competed with the boys in school as if she were one of them. Balanced against this macho personality was the fact that she was and continued to be drop-dead gorgeous in a girl-next-door kind of way. From the time she was a teenager she'd dealt with the advances of men of all ages and never lost her ground. Ms. George was perfectly suited for her career as a law enforcement officer.

She jumped out of bed and headed into the small kitchen which she rarely used except to make coffee or tea. This morning English tea was on her taste buds. The sound of the kettle beginning to boil turned her memory back to her father.

Ariel's mother had died when she was twelve years old — another cancer victim devoured by the enigmatic disease. Her father, Fulton George, was a professor of comparative literature at Yale University for twenty five years before retiring to write and publish his findings on the influence of William Blake upon the poets of the Romantic school, in particular Percy Bysshe Shelley. She couldn't help but smile each time she thought about her father telling her the story that when she was born the name 'Ariel' had come to him as if by magic.

Ariel was the name Shelley had given to the small sail boat he utilized while in Italy at the end of his brief life — the same craft he would die in one stormy day at sea. The vessel had represented freedom to Shelley. Fulton George wanted his daughter to have the same freedom in her life; to do as she wished and make the best of it. But, a career with the FBI had not been in her father's dreams for his daughter's freedom.

She sipped the tea slowly while checking her cell phone to see if she had any messages from the Bureau. Her eyes gazed around the small apartment she had occupied for nearly five years. There were still unpacked boxes. She stared at her suitcase in the middle of the living room floor. Today she was off to Europe on assignment to a U.S. embassy in France. The terrorists of the world kept Ariel in constant motion.

Suddenly she realized how peaceful and quiet it was at five-thirty a.m. on Beacon Hill. There was no movement on the ancient cobblestone streets and her building seemed devoid of life. In the quiet of the moment she remembered the day that she told her father she had been recruited by the FBI. All fatherly pride disappeared from his expression: he looked as if he'd seen a ghost. She knew what he was thinking. He had raised her on his own since she was twelve and now, ten years later, she was contemplating a life in harm's way — a life of danger with the possibility of being killed in the line of duty. At that moment he had grabbed her, hugged her and began to cry. She comforted him as best she could, but the next day she signed on with the Bureau.

She returned her teacup to the kitchen ignoring the dirty dishes in the sink, and finished packing. By nine o'clock she was ready to go to the Boston Bureau for her final briefing and then off to the airport for her flight to Paris.

A light drizzle had begun as the cab was leaving the curb. Ariel George stared out the window as the streets crawled by and wondered casually, what if…Shelley had not loved sailing?

CHAPTER TWENTY-THREE

Twenty-Three

The young boy Niccolo had always been fascinated by his father. He could sit and watch him work all day long. He knew that someday a promise would be kept and he would have his own set of hammers and chisels. Niccolo would laugh out loud when his father returned home from his studio covered in white powder looking like a benevolent ghost.

Antonius Petrarchus was a well-respected artist; a sculptor whose massive mounds of Italian marble were transformed magically before his son's eyes into works of extraordinary beauty.

It was 1955 and Niccolo had just turned thirteen when his father took him and his mother to see their new home. It was late spring in Nice and the weather was warm but the sky was filled with ominous clouds. The family walked in silence towards the old city, "Vieux Nice," with its ancient buildings and endless winding streets. In the maze of yellow, ochre, pink and green structures it was easy to become lost.

They arrived at the plaza of the Palais de Justice and paused in one of the bistros to have a little treat. Niccolo sipped his favorite drink, Orangina, whose fuzzy bubbles tickled his nose. His father and mother held hands while sipping Italian coffee. When they finished, Antonius led them down Rue de la Prefecture. This street was sandwiched between the massive palace on the left and the Cours Salaya, the open flower market on the right, a few steps from the Promenade des Anglais and the Mediterranean Sea.

Antonius stopped and gestured with his beaming smile towards a building at the end of the block. To Niccolo, the structure seemed unimpressive when compared to their current home. No, thought the boy, there must be something wrong here. This building of four stories and pale yellow in color has no balconies or colorful tiles. There was only a plaque on the wall. His mother told him that it was about the death of someone famous who had once lived there. The sculptor proudly announced to his family that their home and his studio would be here, where so many famous artists such as Marc Chagall and the writer Tolstoy had lived and worked. The family would have two floors of the building. Niccolo's mother was overjoyed at the prospect of their new spacious quarters.

"But father," the boy said almost in tears, "Someone has died in this place. Maybe their ghost is still haunting the rooms and runs around at night trying to frighten everyone!"

Antonius laughed from deep inside which made his eyes sparkle and his thick moustache jiggle up and down. He embraced his son with great affection. "There are no worries for us my boy. The man who died here was even more famous than your father. Besides, he was a great musician, and do you know what my son?" Niccolo stared into his father's deep blue eyes. "This great man had your name. That's right, his name was Niccolo — Niccolo Paganini. You are his namesake and he would never even dream of scaring you or making you unhappy."

With these words Niccolo's mother squatted down to give him a big hug. Just the fragrance of her perfume made everything seem right.

Antonius gazed dreamily at their new home. "Just as soon as the alterations are completed and the workers have removed the flooring on the second level so there will be room for my big slabs of marble, we shall move in. I'd say that in one month we will be able to swim in the sea every day. Won't that be great my son?"

Niccolo grinned at his father but couldn't make the specter of a ghost disappear.

Twenty-Four

It was day seven in the mountain cabin. Gus woke up with his right arm killing him. Maria's head had been resting in the cavity of his shoulder since they fell asleep last night after making love. Gus couldn't remember the last time he'd spent a full night with a woman in his arms. His life of womanizing had been just that: a bevy of one-nighters in L.A. or Vegas along with classy hookers who came with the turf in his life style. His philosophy of work and women was the same: sneak in, get the goods — sneak out.

Gus sat up in bed and began an eye-search for his boxers. He grabbed his smokes and watched Maria sleeping. Gus was never comfortable with intimacy. He needed his space. His security blanket was not being needed. To move out on a dime with no goodbyes was his anti-anxiety insurance.

But last night was different. Gus had participated in every combination of sexual experience including two or three women at a time. It usually took a lot to get him going, but when Maria began to slowly unbutton her blouse after her second whisky, Gus almost made her stop. He was feeling something beyond desire. By the time the last button was loose and she peeled her blouse off of her shoulders, Gus wanted her badly in every way imaginable. Before he could make a move she stood up and pulled off her jeans and tossed them across the room. She then knelt in front of him and began to rub his legs while staring into his eyes with a look of pure passion. Her bra and panties were an intricate pattern in black lace. Her nipples grew hard beneath the cups of her bra and Gus felt like he was going to explode. Then she began to message his groin. He was already aroused beyond belief. He leaned back until his body could go no farther into the couch. She unzipped his pants, never taking her eyes off his. She began to kiss, lick and caress him in a way so gentle and at the same time so sensual that he came almost immediately. Gus started to get angry but Maria just laughed and said, "We have all night my love. That was just for starters." Her smile was reassuring and Gus relaxed as the night carried them both away.

He went downstairs to make a pot of coffee. Even a night in the arms of an Italian goddess could not erase his paranoia. Everything seemed still. He opened the front door. Only the sound of water flowing downstream and the wind blowing through the pines could be heard. Sipping his coffee he glanced out of the windows. His eyes scanned the premises like an Alsatian watch dog. He heard feet on the stairs. Maria eased her way down wearing nothing but one of Gus's button-down collar dress shirts. He couldn't figure it out. Why in the hell were women so sexy in a man's long sleeve shirt? To hell with Victoria's Secret, nothing could arouse him as much as the image in front of him.

He poured himself another cup and waved it in her direction while uttering the only phrase he had picked up in Italian since he arrived. "Buon giorno," he smiled proudly, "toast with your coffee or straight for the starter?"

Maria sauntered over to him without saying a word and put

her sleepy arms around his neck and cooed "good morning" in English. Her first words were raspy and she cleared her throat mid-sentence. "I will take just a coffee for now and have you for dessert." She hugged him then kissed him on the cheek and shuffled towards the stove.

Watching her from the back as she poured her first cup of the day Gus knew he was hooked. But as sweet as the moment was, his thoughts turned towards their predicament.

There didn't appear to be any immediate danger from the mysterious stranger which they were sure was following them from day one. Gus was reluctant to let his guard down, but their location was secure and no one had shown up in a week. Maybe they could enjoy themselves and just keep a vigilant eye out.

Maria had been doing her job. As musically ignorant as Gus was, he could hear the difference in the sound of the violin. At first it sounded like a toy, but after a few days it was sounding fatter, more like an electric guitar.

Gus could only think of one problem between them at the moment. Since meeting with Signor Sanoni in the forest, Gus and Maria hadn't really talked that much. Maria had become consumed by the fiddle and seemed to be in another world. Their love making contained little conversation.

In the meantime, Gus had fished and explored the area along the stream being careful to not stray too far away. He kept his Glock 7 in his waistband on these excursions. This feeling of new-found bliss was all well and good but Gus had issues. Were Sanoni and Maria lovers at one time? Were they lovers now?

Suddenly a huge explosion rocked the cabin. Maria screamed and ran into Gus's arms. Panic pumped up the adrenaline and without warning torrents of rain burst from above. The roof creaked under the downfall. No sooner had it arrived then it disappeared. They released the tension in their arms but continued to hold each other while listening to the water dripping from the roof and the forest of pines.

68   Art Johnson

Time stood still for a few moments. They kissed in a warm, affectionate way. Gus Happy was feeling like his last name.

Twenty-Five

G.B. Sanoni shuffled around from place to place in his villa just outside Cremona. He nervously adjusted objects d'art before sitting down. It was ten thirty at night and the candles around the dining room flickered in the slight breeze that came from the garden. A bird was singing. He had never noticed any bird song late at night.

He tried not to focus on the current situation, but it was useless. In only one week since the murder of his good friend and partner, Giovanni was reflecting his true age. How tired and drawn he looked, shocked by the years that seemed to suddenly creep up on him.

He began to collect himself. He removed the envelope from his briefcase which Maria had given him in the forest. Trusting her as he did, he didn't check the contents. He knew there was fifty thousand Euros in five hundred Euro denominations. It was his best fee to date and he deserved it. This copy of Paganini's violin could not be topped.

It was now time to make a plan. His informant at the police

station told him that two American FBI agents would be arriving to interview him. They were sure to question him about his relationship with the deceased Como. It was too late to disappear. These government officials could have no idea about the copy he had made for Max Pendleton.

Within the haze of wine he'd been sipping all night he remembered that his police informant said there were eye-witnesses who saw a man entering and leaving the building around the time of the murder. Perhaps that is why the FBI comes to Cremona. Maybe this suspect is on their most wanted list? Yes, that must be it. Giovanni began to breathe a little easier. There can be nothing to worry about, he thought. This interview should be strictly routine. He must remain calm. There is no reason to panic.

All of the candles burned out except one. G.B. Sanoni took another glance in the mirror as he polished off the last drops of wine. In the flickering light he looked young again. He studied his face for a few moments then blew out the last candle.

His last thoughts for the evening were of Maria. She was his angel and he must do everything to protect her. She meant the world to him.

Twenty-Six

Alistair Krupp had changed his name so many times that once in a bar in Prague, after five straight shots of Polish vodka he couldn't remember his real one. This memory brought about a chuckle from a man who rarely ever laughed as he was dressing for dinner in Milan. He had purchased a new wardrobe and was admiring himself in the full length mirror of his hotel suite.

Gathering up his room key, cell phone and wallet, he swept the room with his eyes and in a last minute gesture, grabbed all of the black clothing strewn across the bed and tossed them into the closet shutting the door.

Alistair was travelling with three passports and several untraceable credit cards. His personal history simply did not exist in computer banks or little black books. He never met his clients and his fees were not negotiable. Cyber café connections or disposable cell phones filled the need for all business communications. He had no friends.

Alistair Krupp spent his life taking the lives of others. The dollar, Rand, Swiss Franc or Euro dictated the total scope of his allegiance. He often saluted the flag of any number of private banks he visited to check his safety deposit boxes.

He entered the elevator and pressed the button for the lobby. There was a couple holding hands standing behind him. They smelled of money and appeared to be in their mid-sixties. When the cabin arrived Alistair held the door to let them pass. They smiled. Alistair felt the man brush up against him as he exited. The pair moved rapidly through the lobby and were quickly out of sight.

Alistair felt inside his coat pocket and found a piece of folded paper. He paused near a palm tree and read the brief message. "It is to our mutual benefit to talk — contact me: Parker."

Walking out into the evening air, he burned the note and hailed a cab. A trickle of sweat ran down his neck. He gave the driver twenty euro to drop him off at the back of the hotel. He walked through the service entrance to take an elevator near the loading docks.

He returned to his suite unnoticed and packed hurriedly while wiping down the room. As soon as he was convinced there were no traces of his presence left behind, he went to the lobby and checked out. He requested a piece of hotel stationary and wrote a quick note to be dropped into the message box of Mr. and Mrs. Parker. The corporate smile of the desk clerk replied, "…Let's see, oh yes, Mr. and Mrs. Jonathan Parker, suite 312. I'll make sure they get your note."

Alistair made his way through the marble-pillared lobby and blended into the night.

Twenty-Seven

A typical fog laden morning engulfed San Diego International Airport as agents Clarke and Gonzales boarded their flight. A day later Chris and Chubbs found themselves on the front steps of police headquarters in Cremona. The warm mid-morning August air was dry and the sun was beginning to bake the city.

Clarke's mind was on the interview about to take place with G.B. Sanoni. Chris had arranged for a translator to be present. Agents Clarke and Gonzales were escorted to a compact interview room painted the universal industrial green, with no windows and one table with four chairs. Already seated was Signor Sanoni, poised in a relaxed manner.

With nearly two decades of sizing up suspects, Chris made a quick evaluation of G.B. Sanoni. He appeared to be intelligent as a craftsman might be, and also gentle by nature. The soul of a true artisan shone in his face and particularly in the eyes.

"Signor Sanoni, I am FBI Special Agent Chris Clarke and this is Agent Carlos Gonzales. We have arrived from the U.S. to investigate the murder of Giuseppe Como. Do you speak or understand English? If not…"

Chris was interrupted by a wave of Sanoni's delicate hand. "I learned the English language many years ago because of my work. You would be surprised by the number of customers coming from America and Great Britain to Italy for violin repairs and to purchase instruments."

Chris took out a digital recorder and placed it on the table. When he returned his eyes to Sanoni the man spoke. "Giuseppe Como was a dear friend, almost, how you say, like a son to me. I do whatever I can to help you find this murderer."

Chris asked him if he would like an attorney present but he declined. "Signor Sanoni, can you tell us what the appointment with the victim was concerning the day he was killed?"

The Italian craftsman's eyes focused on the table top before he replied. "Giuseppe called me earlier in the week to tell me his violin was having a problem with the sound. Do you know anything about violins Agent Clarke?"

"A friend of mine back in California is a violinist with the symphony. He visits the local violin shop regularly for what he calls adjustments."

Sanoni beamed at Chris. "Well then you understand. Giuseppe needed an adjustment on his violin for the sound. That was the reason for our appointment."

Chubbs took over. "Mr. Sanoni, you are employed by a violin maker named Marcel Wittenberg, is that correct?"

Sanoni shifted in his chair and nodded in the affirmative.

Chubbs continued. "Then can you tell us why Mr. Como didn't bring his violin to the shop where you work?"

G.B. Sanoni clasped his hands together tightly. "Well, you see, there was a little problem between Signor Wittenberg and Giuseppe over a charge for repairs that Giuseppe never paid because he didn't think it was fair. You know, he felt cheated so he never returned to the shop. Como liked my work so I invite him to my home. I keep a set of tools there for things like this. It is a little free lance work, but I keep records and pay all the taxes."

Chris and Chubbs glanced at each other. They both noticed a bit of sweat forming on Sanoni's forehead. Chubbs continued. "According to the police report, you arrived at Mr. Como's apartment before calling the police. Is that correct?"

Without hesitation Sanoni responded. "That's right. I went there then I called the police."

Chubbs locked onto Sanoni's eyes. "Weren't you tempted to go inside, to see if your friend was injured in some way?"

"Well, I knock on the door but no one comes. I try the door but she is locked, so I wait."

Chubbs stared into his BlackBerry before continuing. "Did the police have to break the door down or did they have a key?"

G.B. Sanoni smiled as he replied. "The police have keys that fit most old apartments in Cremona. Nothing changes much here. The Italian life overall moves slowly. People try to enjoy each day. Old lock, new lock, she's about the same." The violin craftsman took a deep breath as if he had just imparted the secret of life. Maybe he had, Chris thought as he took back the reins.

"Tell us Signor Sanoni, can you think of any person that may have wished to kill Giuseppe Como? Did he have any jealous girlfriends, or other musicians that might wish him harm?"

Sanoni became pensive. "Everyone loved Giuseppe. He had only friends and admirers. His girlfriend Valerie, she cries all the time I hear. No Signor inspector, I can think of no one who would do such a thing."

Chris called for a break. He left the room to check up on the interview with Valerie Allesandro. She had been with Giuseppe the previous night but had left his apartment early in the morning to go to her job at the museum. Witnesses confirmed her location at work during the estimated time of Como's demise. Chris headed back to the cramped interview room. Down the hallway he could smell cigarette smoke. For the first time in over a year, he felt like lighting up.

Chris thought that the man was telling the truth, just not all of it. Chubbs switched on the recorder and Chris followed his intuition. "Tell me, Signor Sanoni, in your lifetime of restoring and repairing violins, haven't you ever been tempted to build your own?"

Giovanni cleared his throat. "Of course, in my early studies it is a requirement in the school to build a violin so you can prove you know every part. Did you know Signor Inspector that there are over seventy parts in each violin?"

Chris's voice became more intense. "What did you do with this violin you built so many years ago? Do you still have it?"

Sanoni fidgeted in his chair. "No, she was no good. Some parts I use for repairing other violins and the rest I just throw away."

Chris knew he was closer to a secret. "Well Signor Sanoni, my partner and I have travelled a good ways to talk to you today and I must admit, you leave us quite confused." Sanoni froze.

Chris moved closer. "You see, we've checked your bank account and also that of Giuseppe Como's. There seems to be a recurring feature to both. Every two months or so, you withdraw one to three thousand euros and the next day Como deposits a like sum. So it stands to reason that this money is a fee or commission of some kind. Surely your boss Marcel Wittenberg would not approve of you selling instruments away from the shop, so my mind searches for the reason that these sums exchange hands?" Sanoni was drenched in sweat. "You see Signor Sanoni, I have this way of seeing things like little pictures in my mind and amazing results occur sometimes."

Sanoni went defensive. "Excuse me Signor Clarke, I do not understand what you mean."

Chris pressed. "Oh, I think you do. Why don't you tell us about the little work shop you have hidden away, where you fashion replicas of the great masters, Amati, Stradivarius and Guarneri by commission?"

Sanoni's face went blank. It was if a computer had just crashed. His lips began to tremble.

"You see," continued Chris, "I find it impossible for any human being with such a talent as yours to deny yourself the pleasure of creating fine instruments. In searching for a motive for the murder of your young friend I have a theory that at the center of this tragedy there must be a violin; a very important violin."

Sanoni broke into tears. The flow was unstoppable. Chris was patient. He let the man sob his heart out. The old man finally spoke. "I did not want anyone to get hurt. I just love the violin." Sanoni stared at Chris. "I get a commission to make a copy of Paganini's violin which is in the museum in Genoa. The client wants it to be the best copy ever made and he offers me my biggest fee ever."

Chubbs jumps in. "And you had hired Giuseppe to break in the fiddle as you had in the past with your other copies?"

"Yes, yes." Sanoni said these words as if all life had been drained out of him.

Chubbs demanded. "We need to know the name of the client and all contact information."

Sanoni held up his arms up in frustration. "I never see or meet the client. I find a letter under the door of my home. It contains a proposal and how much money I get."

Chris broke in. "How did your client check on the work in progress?"

G.B. Sanoni was hyper-ventilating. "One day I get a call on my cell phone and it's him. He calls me two other times and then I finish the violin and leave it near a tree in the forest south of here. My money is in a bag at my front door when I return."

Chris asked, "Didn't you check your cell phone to trace the caller's number?"

Sanoni chirped. "I check but it is blank. Caller ID blocked."

Chubbs reflected in silence for a moment then asked, "Tell

me, why all this secrecy Signor Sanoni, why all this intrigue over building a musical instrument?"

Sanoni caught his breath. "It is the mystery of the violin itself. The violin world is not like the everyday world of most people. It is a society full of skilled dreamers and deceivers."

As the violin maker was being escorted out of the room he paused by Chris. "Tell me, how did you know about my workshop? Somebody told you? You've been here before?"

Chris faced Sanoni. "You told me with your eyes the minute I saw you."

The two FBI agents concluded their interview and requested that the police hold G.B. Sanoni in custody for twenty four hours as a key witness. It was not illegal to make a violin for sale to an anonymous client, but Chris didn't believe his story about the invisible man.

Before Chris and Chubbs left the station, the witnesses who had seen a "man in black" at the scene of the crime arrived to be interviewed. Two of them, a mother and her daughter, had been on their balcony watering sun-drenched plants. They noticed a man of average build moving swiftly away from the complex. They thought it was way too hot to be dressed completely in black. The third witness was a Cremona businessman who had his front door open while talking to a client on his cell phone. He saw the stranger entering the building. He was dressed in black and smoking a small cigar. It happened so fast he was not sure he could identify him again.

Agents Clarke and Gonzales stepped out into the late afternoon sunlight. Chubbs turned to Chris. "Hey partner, do you think the old man really had anything to do with the killing?"

Chris caught a whiff of cigarette smoke. "No," he sighed, "but I believe that Sanoni's copy is at the bottom of this mess. My gut feeling tells me that there is a plan underway to steal the original and replace it with the copy. I think we'll get more info out of

Sanoni after he spends the night in the tank."

Chris paused. "We've earned some R and R; let's grab some pasta and wine. Sound good?"

"That's a big 10-4 oh mighty one." Chubbs grinned.

They headed for the heart of the old city, stopping briefly at a tobacco shop on the way.

Twenty-Eight

The man in the light blue jogging suit, sporting wrap-around sunglasses and a Yankee baseball cap squatted down to re-lace his Nikes. He was prepared to run if necessary.

His note to Jonathan Parker was brief and to the point: "garden opposite hotel, first bench near fountain -2:00 pm – Sunday." Alistair would jog around the park looking every bit the tourist and hover near the bench just before the hour.

He had done his homework at a local cyber café. When he Googled Parker he discovered a complete bio including his respected skills as a concert violinist. The question still remained. How did the Parkers discover his identity, location and what he was planning?

Alistair reached inside the pocket of his jacket and fondled the small, custom made graphite .38 caliber hand gun equipped with a silencer. He felt that tingle of confidence.

Just before two o'clock he jogged past the well-tended flower beds on the lip of the park and headed along the path leading to the bench. He slowed down as he recognized Jonathan Parker already seated reading a newspaper. The smiling stranger folded his paper and beckoned Alistair to join him as if they were old friends. Jonathan patted the space on the bench next to him and Alistair sat down. Curiosity was taking over the assassin's consciousness. Alistair silently flicked off the safety catch on his pistol.

As if he were reading his mind, Jonathan spoke. "Did you notice the withered grandmother with the baby carriage seated on the bench behind us? That's my wife. Damn good shot at any range, particularly this close." Alistair expressed a tight-lipped smile. Jonathan smiled back. "I will not waste either of our time. I am here to assist you in your current goal. It is up to you to decide if my assistance is of any value."

Alistair took over. "I'm not sure how you found out about me or what you have in mind, but make it quick. You have about two minutes to explain yourself before I make a decision about your future, granny and all."

"Fair enough," Jonathan replied. "You are in pursuit of an object which has been a part of your heritage for nearly two centuries. Through your sources you discovered that two thieves were planning to remove and replace this object from the museum in Genoa. You murdered a violinist who was part of the plan thinking that it would scare everyone off. You were wrong."

Jonathan could feel the cold steel eyes behind dark glasses. "You're running out of time, old man," Alistair said impatiently, "get to the point!"

"Fine," Jonathan returned. "You want your thrice-great grandfather's violin and I merely desire the original box that housed it. Yes, I know you are the distant grandson of Niccolo Paganini's son Achilles. How I know is my business. What I can say for sure is that those involved will attempt to switch it within the next few days."

Alistair pondered the stranger's face. "Tell me friend, why in the hell should the original violin box be of such interest to you? It can't be worth enough to a man of your obvious financial means, so what gives?"

Jonathan responded enigmatically. "My reasons are personal and at the same time universal. Suffice it to say that I have no interest in the violin itself but am prepared to help you acquire it as long as I get the box. Are you interested?"

"Well," Alistair answered, "it's your move and it had better be good for your sake."

Before their discussion continued, Jonathan signaled with a nod of his head and the grandmother behind him moved away, leaving an empty baby carriage behind.

Twenty-Nine

After twelve days in the mountain cabin Maria decided that the violin was sounding as it should and that it was time to return to Parma to regroup.

The genius of G.B. Sanoni never ceased to amaze her. Through all the years of the violin in her life it was still his instruments that remained special. His magical boxes beckoned you to escape into the mystery of their sound.

In the past two weeks of playing the Devil's copy, she believed that this was Signor Sanoni at his best. The violin seemed full of experience and the toil of centuries in her hands. The glow of the varnish cast shadows from the past.

Gus helped her pack up and secure the cabin. He paused on the porch to take a deep breath of mountain air and closed his eyes. Maria wrapped her arms around him from behind. "You will miss our peaceful beginnings Signor Gus?" Gus turned and embraced her as if she were about to slip away.

Before he knew it they were back at the apartment in Parma.

Gus reclined on the sofa and watched Maria stare into the computer screen. She printed out something and pounced onto his lap. "We are in luck," she said while waving a piece of paper in the air above their heads. "The museum in Genoa is presenting a concert featuring an American violinist playing the Devil's violin. It's next Monday. We can drive down and check things out. Sound good?"

Gus pulled away from Maria and grabbed a smoke while gathering his thoughts. He knew what he needed to say but he would only have one chance and he'd better be right.

"Look," he said exhaling, "I'm not the perfect person with words where feelings are involved. I know that since we've been together someone has been following us. I think he murdered your friend in Cremona. I expected him while we were at the cabin but he never surfaced. I'm not sure how he fits into this mess, but one thing is for sure, all this shit is due to this violin and I wish to hell I'd never answered the phone when Max called." He paused to flick an ash into an empty coffee cup. Maria stared at him barely moving a muscle. "But on the other hand, if I hadn't come to Parma I would never have met you and…shit, I don't know what the hell I'm trying to say."

Maria put her finger to his lips and whispered, "I am the same way as you. I am worried and madly in love at the same time. It is difficult — no?"

Gus tightened up. "There is something I need to know before we make another move." Gus paused to make sure he had her full attention. "The old man, that Sanoni character, what the hell is he to you? Is he an ex-lover or husband or what? You two seemed a bit too intimate that day in the forest."

Maria walked over to open the French windows. She stood facing the September sun. "I tell you quite frankly Gus, I love that man very deeply, but not for the reasons you are thinking."

Gus shot up from the couch. "Just great, tell me all about him."

"Gus," Maria said as she turned to face him, "have you ever wondered what my last name is? You never asked, even once."

The realization startled him. "Jesus Christ, I never thought to ask."

Maria moved over and clasped his hands. "My last name is Sanoni. G.B. Sanoni is my father. My mother died when I was four years old. He raised me by himself and gave me the world of the violin. This discipline and enchantment helped to fill the emptiness."

Gus felt like shit. Was he really that big a jerk? Why had he gone for the jugular instead of thinking for one minute that the old man might be her father? He collapsed on the couch and searched for some way to apologize but no thoughts were able to form into words.

It reminded him of the day when he found out his mother had died of a sudden heart attack. At the time he was in Vegas shooting craps. Emotion swelled up inside but nothing came out. He took a deep breath after closing his cell phone and rolled the dice: snake eyes.

CHAPTER THIRTY

The atmosphere in the concert hall was heavy. The anticipation throughout the audience to hear the most famous violin in the world was intense. Gus and Maria bought some of the last tickets. Their seats were on folding chairs in the back of the room. Gus began to squirm and fidget before the concert began. Maria grabbed his hand. "Relax my love, after the concert there is a viewing. It is very important for me to see the instrument up close."

Gus was about to ask her why when the musicians took the stage and tuned up. Throughout the performance Gus couldn't focus on the music. His time was consumed by keeping an eye out for the enemy.

The final notes sounded and the audience shot to their feet yelling bravo. Gus and Maria left the concert hall to return to the museum to be first in line to view the violin. When they arrived at the Palazzo Tursi they were escorted into a small room that held around fifty persons. The viewing would be done in shifts. Armed guards with expressionless faces were close by as a bald man in a tuxedo stood at attention behind a table. He put on a pair of white gloves and slowly held the violin up for people to see. Maria was within two feet of the prize. She examined as much detail as possible. She asked the exhibitor a few questions and requested to see the back of the violin. The man rotated the fiddle. Gus didn't understand Italian, but at one point Maria said something and the man burst out laughing, almost dropping the violin.

They left the museum with Maria consumed in thought. It was as if she were alone.

"You certainly cracked that guy up in there. What did you say to him?"

Maria stopped walking and gave Gus a peck on the cheek. "Oh, I just told him how beautiful the violin was and that it was a shame that it was a fake."

Gus gasped. "You've got to be kidding me, right?"

Maria let out one of her patented giggles. "No my darling, for many years I've been researching and sorting through the clues."

Gus broke a cigarette trying to light it. "Clues, what in the hell are you talking about baby? You telling me we've been wasting our time and there is no job to do?"

Maria grabbed Gus's arm tight enough to cause pain. "Yes, there is still a job to do, but it's not here in Italy. We must go to Nice where the Devil died." Maria guided Gus to a nearby park bench. "I know that you have wondered about the large leather bound books in my office, yes?" Gus nodded. "These books are collections of documents handed down for over one hundred and fifty years. Violin making goes back three generations in my family. My grandfather and my father had a shop together when I was a child. I spent hours there each day. While reading through piles of old documents concerning Paganini, I found a curious letter meant for his son Achilles. It was written near the time he died. The envelope was still sealed after all these years. In this letter he refers to the copy of his violin and begins to explain a plan which is never finished. Perhaps Paganini was too ill to complete the message." Maria laughed, Gus looked confused. "My father derives much joy from telling the story of the fake Guarneri crafted by J.B. Vuillaume in Paris that even fooled Paganini. When I saw the violin today I knew it was the copy. There are slight markings on the back to distinguish it from the real one." Gus looked like he was going to pass out. Maria continued.

"My great grandfather discovered a letter while in Toulouse in 1860. It was for J.B. Vuillaume's brother, also a violin maker. He tells him about the fun he had fooling the great Paganini and describes the cryptic markings on the fake that sets it apart."

Gus's head was spinning. Now he was confronting violin detective, Nancy Drew, who seemed to be more out of her mind than when he met her. He maintained his patience.

"So, what you're telling me is that the real fiddle is probably in France, but you're guessing, right? I mean, you think it's there because when you were a kid you dreamed about it being there so now were off to Nice to see if you're right or wrong — right?"

Gus wasn't sure what he'd said when he finished. Fortunately Maria was paying attention.

"I am not a little girl dreaming. Give me more credit than that! We still have a job to do. I think we shall find the real Devil's violin where Paganini died. If the copy is in the museum then the original must still be in Nice. Paganini must have hidden it before he died: maybe in his apartment. We must go there and within a few days we'll know."

As Maria began to explain the details of her plan, Gus attempted to relieve his stress by wondering if French fries were invented in France.

Thirty-One

Chubbs adjusted the rear view mirror of the rented Ford Focus as he settled into the driver's seat. They were off to Genoa. The museum which displays the prized violin had just hosted a special performance and viewing of the instrument two days ago. Appointments had been made to interview the museum staff.

They entered the auto route heading south. "Wow chief, Sanoni sure folded fast when you told him you thought another family member was involved."

Chris was spaced out due to fatigue. "When I asked him if he had any children his mouth twitched. I just took a stab in the dark when I told him I knew all about his daughter."

Chubbs checked the GPS. "How did you know she played the violin?"

Chris adjusted his seat belt. "It stood to reason that with the violin at the core of the guy's life that his kid would be a maker or a player. With a daughter the odds are that she'd be a player."

Chubbs concentrated on the drive. "What do you think we'll find in Genoa?"

Chris gazed at the Tuscan countryside. "My guess is that whoever has the copy may have already made the switch or is about to do so. The murder of Giuseppe Como may have changed things. She and her partner may have called it off, I can't really guess on that one."

Chubbs shot a quick glance at his passenger. "What's this 'she' thing? You think his daughter is one of those involved?"

Chris reached into his pocket for a pack of cigarettes which weren't there. "If my gut feeling is correct the answer is yes. If the 'man in black' is the third piece of the puzzle and we follow the thieves who are after the violin, we might just get our man."

Chris was drowsy. His mind was shutting down. He thought about Brenda and the kids. He hadn't seen them for so long. He prevented himself from thinking about them because of the pain. At this moment memories seemed to vanish like the Italian landscape along the auto route. All the scenery passed by with no purpose, nothing to cling to.

Once in Genoa, they headed for the museum. Chris felt that time was critical. He was anxious to interview the gentleman who had conducted the viewing after the concert. Chubbs would gather the other employees that were on hand that afternoon and question them with an interpreter.

Chris was introduced to the museum curator, Signor Abramo Contesso. He was a wide-eyed man around fifty years of age, slightly rotund with a balding head, a well cropped mustache and a gracious manner. He spoke English with a heavy accent. Chris thought of Hercule Poirot.

"Tell me, how was the concert Monday night?" Chris smiled at Abramo.

"The American virtuoso Josh Bell, he play *magnifico!*" Signor Contesso kissed his fingertips. "The whole concert is beautiful music."

Chris moved forward. "Can you tell me about the viewing

afterwards. Isn't that a bit unusual?"

Abramo straightened his back. "In the ten years I have worked here, there has only been one other public viewing."

"Was there a large crowd?"

Abramo smiled proudly. "Oh, *si* Signor Clarke, maybe two hundred or more come to see the magic violin. I personally conduct the showing and believe me it is a very big responsibility. I handle the violin with gloves. I must be very careful."

Chris nodded understandingly. "Do people ask a lot of questions?"

Abramo cleared his throat. "Yes, but many people just stare with their eyes big like children."

Chris pressed on. "Tell me Signor Contesso, can you remember anything unusual or any person or persons who stood out?"

The museum curator held his chin between his thumb and first finger and explored his memory. "Well, there was a lot questions, you know, what kind of wood it's made out of, how old is it, and how much she's worth. Those are pretty much the normal inquiries, but there was this beautiful Signora, she was a real knock out, who asked me to turn the violin over so she could see the back. She looked a long time with her big eyes, then she said something to me which makes me laugh so hard I almost drop the treasure."

A rush of adrenalin shot through Chris. "What did she say that was so amusing?"

"After she examined the back of the violin very slowly she tells me it's a beautiful violin, too bad it's a fake! I almost fall over."

Chris felt he was getting close. "Tell me Signor Abramo, was she alone or with someone?"

The curator thought for a moment. "Yes, there was a man with her, an American. He was average height and had blonde curly hair. He doesn't say anything like he's not interested at all."

Chris thanked Signor Contesso and concluded the interview. He sought out Chubbs to compare notes. They requested that the local police check all the hotels in the area to see if a couple fitting the description given by the museum had booked a room around the day of the concert.

If the violin in the museum is a fake according to Maria Sanoni, then where is the real item? Is she on the trail to find the real Devil's violin? Was "the man in black" in the picture?

Walking to the hotel to grab a bite and get some rest, Chris took a detour into another tobacco shop.

Thirty-Two

One thing was worrying Maria. She had tried to call her father on his cell phone and had not been able to reach him. When she and Gus arrived back in Parma there was an envelope leaning against the front door. Maria snatched it up. She recognized her father's delicate script. She read the letter and moved like a ghost into the front room and collapsed on the couch.

Gus sat opposite her. "What's up baby? Is that from your dad?" It seemed to Gus that she didn't hear him. He was about to repeat the question when she spoke up.

"Yes, my father has been in jail for two days." She darted around the room searching for a cigarette. "Two FBI agents arrived from the US to interrogate him about Giuseppe. One of the agents figured out that he had made a copy of the Guarneri and that his daughter plays the violin."

"Gee," Gus shouted, "did your father also tell them all about me — my hair color and shirt size?" Reality was sidelining all romantic fantasies. "Look." He snorted, "Life is tough enough in this business without leaving bread crumbs behind for the police to follow." Gus could feel his blood pressure on the rise, "I know for a fact that this whole fucking thing has gotten completely out of control and we now have about one chance in a hundred of not getting our necks in a noose before this is over."

In an instant, Maria rushed over and plunged into Gus's lap, wrapped her arms around him and began to cry. His first inclination was to get boiling mad but he couldn't make himself do it. Without thinking he held on to her for dear life. They passed several minutes in this silent embrace and finally Maria spoke.

"We must move quickly and take the train to Nice. It will be the safest way to travel. No car to trace. It will only take two or three days to discover the truth." Maria glanced at Gus with a pleading look. "I need you Gus. I can't do this without you."

Gus lit a cigarette. "Did I ever tell you how much I hate trains?"

Thirty-Three

The Mistral arrived at the beginning of September on the Cote d'Azur. Hot, dry winds from the west were living up to their reputation. Nice was like a desert. The whipping currents of air were everywhere. Even the narrow winding labyrinth of streets in the old city could not escape. Clay flower pots on window sills blew over crashing onto the cobble stone.

The sea along the Promenade des Anglais was dotted with white caps. The heat was intense but few were brave enough to fight the waves and enter the water to cool off.

Sculptor, Niccolo Petrarchus brushed away the marble dust from his clothing. The Mistral aided him. Although his studio on Rue Niepce in central Nice was spacious, when he was close to finishing a piece, he would pull the heavy marble onto the street in a hand cart to examine his work in natural light. His latest creation was that of a nude female kneeling on one knee with her arms in supplication, fingertips pointed towards the heavens.

The son of Antonius Petrarchus ran his eyes from top to bottom as he slowly circled his creation several times. The proportions were accurate. Well honed, perfect in symmetry, but there was no life, no soul emanating from his work.

His father had patiently taught him the craft as soon as he was able to wield a mallet and chisel. Antonius had much enthusiasm for his son's potential talent. The old man was able to discover the image hidden within the stone before the first strike of the hammer. He had hoped that this vision would be passed along.

Niccolo knew that he did not share his father's gift. The child of a famous artist knows that throughout his life he will live in the shadow of his parent. He would never surpass or even equal his father's genius. However, these insights did not upset Niccolo or depress him. He knew he owed his father everything he was today.

He walked back into his studio moving past the office where his much younger Japanese wife sat calmly writing checks for the bills. Hopefully, a new commission or a batch of students would arrive soon.

Niccolo paused in front of a metal door which guarded the room full of virgin marble blocks. He entered. Even in this heat wave the massive chunks of stone were cool to the touch. One block of marble sat alone. It contained a great secret: the treasure his father had found in the flooring of their new apartment fifty years ago. He closed the door and set the special alarm unique to this room.

His father had bequeathed to him a fortune that could not be spent: a magnificent voice that must be silent, which Niccolo guarded faithfully, true to his father's last wish.

Thirty-Four

The black BMW with smoked windows exited the main entrance of Paramount Studios. It made a right hand turn on Melrose Avenue heading towards La Cienega Boulevard. The business day was over for this driver. He drove with the air conditioning on freezing, smoking a cigar while consumed in thought. Today's budget deal debates were nothing compared to what was on Max Pendleton's mind at the moment. He pulled into the parking lot of Astro family restaurant on Beverly Boulevard. He dined here when he needed to sort through problems. Today he had a big one.

Max had excused himself earlier in the day from his meeting with the big shots at Paramount to go to the bathroom when his satellite cell phone vibrated in his coat. Only a handful of people had this number. The caller left their code name: "Basta" was for Maria Sanoni. Something must be up. Max called her back and got a clear picture of what had gone down in the past few days. The murder of the violinist was not good for the story. This scene was not in the script. He thought, "Why in the hell did someone eliminate an actor who only had a walk-on part?"

Max was a mover and shaker. Getting himself out of tough situations was a routine affair. The script was going through an unauthorized re-write. It would require a delicate solution. When the competition is unknown it is impossible to control the whole production. Renegade directors are always the toughest to handle.

Max ate his bacon, eggs and biscuits in gravy along with the endless coffee cup slowly as he thought it all through. First of all the FBI is on the scene. Their main concern must be the killer.

It's time to let the badges do their job. Hopefully, Gus and Maria won't forget their lines when the camera starts to roll.

The Hollywood film producer thought about Maria's discovery. The violin in Genoa is a fake. He listened carefully to her plan then encouraged her to go to Nice and find out once and for all if the Devil's violin still exists.

Thirty-Five

Ariel George was due at the American embassy in Nice by ten o'clock. She was to meet up with two Bureau agents who had just arrived from San Diego. Something was up. It was always the same: fear and anticipation, side by side, struggling for supremacy. Her hotel was within walking distance. She bounded down the stairwell and hit the street full of energy five minutes before agents Clarke and Gonzales left their hotel a half a block from the embassy.

Chris and Chubbs were buzzed through to the foyer. Within these four walls they were technically in the United States. A U.S. Marshall told them that the assistant ambassador, Donald Sheldon would be right with them. Chris and Chubbs took a seat and glanced at the headlines of the New York Times.

Chubbs was gleeful. "Hey partner, it sure feels good to be back in the good ole U.S. of A. Did you notice? Right on the corner of our hotel is a huge McDonald's. Man, it sure feels like Big Mac time to me!"

Chris pretended that he hadn't heard a word Chubbs said.

A door opened from the back of the room and out stepped a distinguished looking man in his mid-fifties wearing a pin stripe suit that screamed big bucks. "Agents Clarke...Gonzales, I'm Donald Sheldon, welcome to the United States." The redundant line made Chris's stomach turn.

"We'd like to get started immediately if that's convenient." Chris took an immediate disliking to the assistant ambassador.

In an attempt to conjure wit where none existed, Donald Sheldon replied, "Oh, I see, you must have a plane to catch."

"No, no, nothing like that," Chris replied, "it's just that my partner is dying for a Big Mac and we want to get downstairs before the line gets too long."

Without noticing the barbed remark, the assistant ambassador ushered them towards the conference room. Just then, Ariel George was buzzed through into the foyer and froze in her tracks. Chris spun around and did a double take.

"My God, Chris — is it really you?" FBI Agent George took on the demeanor of a high school cheer leader. "I can't believe it!"

Chris opened his arms and she ran into them. Chubbs remained in place with an ear to ear grin, while Donald Sheldon tried to hide his embarrassment behind an insincere look of surprise.

Chris turned to Chubbs. "Agent Carlos Gonzales, this is Agent Ariel George. We trained together at Quantico. We haven't seen each other in twenty years." Chris beamed at her then came back to earth. "Okay folks, let's get to it."

When the three-some arrived at the conference room they were met by two other agents. Jean-Louis Bernard was with the French Secret Service. He was assigned to the case as part of the Interpol agreement between the U.S. Government and the European Union for jurisdiction by the FBI. Along with Bernard was Pete Shaw, a fellow FBI agent from the Nashville Bureau.

Chris brought everyone up to speed on the current situation and the challenges which lie ahead.

Agent Shaw spread a folder out on the table. "Okay, with the co-operation of the Genoa police at your request Agent Clarke, they ID'd the couple that attended the violin concert at the museum. The female is one, Maria Constantine Sanoni, of Parma Italy. She reads clean on the Bureau's files. The young lady appears to earn her keep as an interior designer and antique dealer.

"Her partner, however, is another story. An American from California, his name is Gustav Edward Happy. He's been arrested twice; once for petty theft fifteen years ago and more recently for grand theft. Mr. Happy never spent more than an overnight in lock up. He has a Beverly Hills attorney named Goldstein who is well connected and squeaky clean. According to immigration he entered Italy around three weeks ago, a few days prior to the murder." Pete Shaw looked at Chris. "Your hunch was right. We found them both here in Nice. They checked into the Hotel Hancy two days ago. Bernard followed them to a real estate office not far from here yesterday. They went and looked at an apartment for sale in the old town." Pete smiled. "Makes me think that they're getting ready to settle down and raise a family."

A mini-second of laughter sprinkled the room. Chris took over. "First of all, my name is Chris and as we're going to be working together for the next few days, let's keep it casual. My partner's nickname is Chubbs for more than obvious reasons." Chubbs smiled, no one laughed. Chris continued. "As we all know, the violin is not the primary focus of this investigation but it may well be the catalyst that brings this case to a conclusion. The "man in black" is definitely involved to some degree in this case. He may have murdered the violinist in Cremona. If it is him, I ask myself why? His MO has always been political. Chris stared off into space for a moment. "I'm not pleased by the fact that I'm not coming up with an answer."

Pete Shaw raised a question. "We've got more fiddles in Nashville than cock roaches. Maybe the man has some psychological fixation about this particular violin. Do you think he killed the kid to scare off the thieves?"

"Good call Pete." Chris finally sat down at the table. "My gut feeling is that our "man in black" is not far behind our lovebirds. I have no idea why he's interested in the violin but it seems to me that if we keep an eye on Gus and Maria that there's a chance he will show up."

Chris turned to Agent George. "Ariel, since it's just after ten o'clock I'd like you to hustle over to the hotel and keep tabs on the movement of Ms. Sanoni. Report back to me every hour. I want to know her every move."

Chris turned to Agents Bernard and Shaw. "I need you two to keep tabs on Gus Happy in case they don't move around as a team today." Both agents nodded in unison.

Chris looked up at the ceiling. "One thing puzzles me. Why did they go look at an apartment in the old town?"

Jean-Louis who had been quiet up to this point spoke up. "Monsieur Clarke I've been waiting to tell you. The building that the apartment is located in is under re-construction. I examined the façade and found a plaque to the left of the entrance. It is written in Italian."

Chris focused his attention. "What did it say?"

The Frenchman adjusted his cravat. "Basically, it was commemorating the death of Niccolo Paganini who died on those premises in 1840, twenty years before Nice became part of France."

Chris demanded. "Jean-Louis, did Maria and Gus Happy do anything else before or after visiting the apartment?"

"Oui, excuse moi Monsieur Clarke, they went to the Hotel de Ville, the hall of records in the center of Nice before they went to the apartment."

"The hall of records," Chris whispered to himself. "Okay, my feeling is we're getting close. In the meantime, Chubbs and I will try to track down more info on our killer. Let's get to it and meet back in my room at five o'clock. Keep me updated throughout the day if anything breaks."

The simultaneous sound of chairs shuffling across the floor signaled the close of their meeting. Chris had a picture of the comely face of Ariel George on his mind. For multiple reasons his pulse was beginning to quicken.

Thirty-Six

Chris had just returned to his hotel room after the meeting when his cell phone went off. "Clarke here…"

"Agent Clarke, Donald Sheldon Calling."

Chris rolled his eyes. "Yes, what can I do for you?"

Sheldon spoke with pompous self-importance clinging to every word. "I truly hate to bother you after your grueling morning but I believe something of great importance occurred at the embassy last night and I think you had better return here tout de suite. I really don't want to say anything more on the phone."

When Chris re-entered the conference room there was a young man sitting at the table dressed almost identically as the ambassador. In front of him was a lap top. He was wearing a smirk on his face while fondling the mouse as if it were a set of rosary beads.

Sheldon beamed at the kid. "Well now, I'm sure that this young man needs no introduction to an FBI associate of your stature Agent Clarke. This is *the* Malcolm S. Turnberry III."

The name, although it seemed familiar wasn't punching through. "Sorry..." Chris furrowed his brow until he remembered. "Right, Malcolm Turnberry, the computer hacker who broke into the Federal Reserve Bank security vault and allocated a few million bucks to his Princeton fraternity pals. That little fiasco earned you a top spot on our most wanted list until you turned yourself in."

Malcolm basked in the light of recognition as if he were a film star who had just been spotted in a crowd.

Chris sat down. "I thought you were doing ten to twenty in a swank Federal lockup outside of D.C.?"

Turnberry shrugged. "The U.S. government decided to give me job rather than waste my skills by chilling me out in prison. Let's just say that it's a win-win situation and I've been assigned here to help out however I can."

Sheldon had the look of a proud father on his face. Chris thought he was going to throw up. "Well, best of luck to one and all. Now, what is so important that you needed me back here?"

Donald Sheldon took the floor. "The embassy is equipped with a twenty-four hour, seven day a week answering system that offers those persons calling to leave a message of any length when we are not here to serve them."

Chris shifted in his chair wondering how long it would take for this pretentious asshole to get to the point.

Sheldon continued. "Last night at eleven thirty two the message you are about to hear came in. Malcolm is responsible for unraveling our little mystery here by applying his special gifts and computer techniques."

Chris thought he was going to explode. "I assume that you've downloaded it onto your lap top, so can you play it for me?"

Malcolm smiled as he slid the computer over to Chris tapping a few buttons in the process. The voice had been altered by some electronic device which made it sound like Darth Vader.

"*If you are looking for the man in black, try researching the name Alistair Krupp."*

Chris punched in Chubbs phone number on his cell and told him to return to the embassy pronto. His eyes searched for an ashtray as he requested to hear the message again. Chris leaned back in his chair and gave Malcolm a long, hard look.

"Got any insight to throw out Mr. Computer Whiz?"

Malcolm stood up and paced the room as he explained. "Okay, first of all I was able to filter the voice through a series of digital voice pattern enhancers. This allowed me, to a certain degree, to reverse the effect of the voice altering tool and return it to its original timbre. The device used to disguise this voice is probably a Radio Shack over-the-counter product sold by the millions over the past forty years after the Star Wars films prompted so much merchandising. Most likely it is impossible to trace the buyer, but that would be your department, eh, Agent Clarke?"

Chris asked to hear the message now that it was scrubbed clean. It was a woman's voice. The door of the conference room flew open and Chubbs entered.

"Have a listen to this." Chris nodded to Malcolm.

Chubbs listened intently. "What is this all about chief?"

Chris smiled at Malcolm. "I think we're about to find out."

Malcolm cleared his throat. "Right…what we seem to have here, according to the technical analysis software I have been able to apply thus far is this: a female, Caucasian, anywhere from forty-five to sixty-five years of age, most likely of North American heritage."

Chris interrupted. "Why do you conclude that she is an American?"

Chubbs jumped in. "How can you be so sure? Are you an expert in racial profiling?"

Malcolm stood in the corner with his hands in his pockets. "That's a fair question. No, I'm not an expert in the field but my software is. I have dozens of voice graph oscillatory maps loaded in my laptop. They analyze regional accents in all languages as well as phrase preferences of every nation. This particular voice imprint, once cleaned up was easy for my tools to define: white, female, middle-aged, with a slight east coast American accent. Of course, I must emphasize the room for error. I'd say that my results are ninety percent accurate."

Malcolm shut the lid of his PC and handed Chris a hard drive disc which contained the original and cleaned up message.

Chris and Chubbs left the embassy with no plan in mind. They wandered across the street drawn by the blue chairs facing the sea on the Promenade des Anglais. When they sat down Chubbs entered the name Alistair Krupp into his BlackBerry and sat motionless. Chris was trying to fit the pieces of the puzzle together as he became mesmerized by the undulating rhythm and the variations of color on the surface of the water.

Who was this woman who casually offered up a name which had eluded the Bureau's finest researchers for over a decade? And furthermore, why did she leave the message?

Chris could hear the sound of skate boards behind him as well as a mix of languages — French, English and Italian — as his gaze swept the horizon. A sharp beep from his cell phone broke his reverie. The sky darkened as clouds passed in front of the sun.

Thirty-Seven

"Chris, its Ariel. I've got some news for you."

Pulling himself out of the fog he searched for a cigarette. "Lay it on me Agent George."

"I followed Maria Sanoni from the hotel a few minutes ago and she walked about a block and a half to an art studio called, *Gallerie Petrarchus*. I waited about five minutes, then walked in with as much tourist on my face as possible. She was asking about art lessons and flirting with the guy like mad."

Chris lit up. "What happened next?"

"Well, I wandered in and took the same brochure for lessons. The sculptor was giving her a tour of the studio. I followed them silently. She was very interested in seeing his storage room where he keeps the virgin slabs of marble."

Chris broke in. "Did you notice anything unusual?"

Ariel said excitedly, "Yes. Petrarchus has a separate code pad for this room. There is an overall standard alarm system for the studio but for some reason, this room gets extra protection. I hung around until she signed up for lessons. After she left I signed up for the same course beginning tomorrow morning."

Chris was picturing Ariel's face. "Stay on it Agent George and good work. I'll see you at five for the meeting."

Chris closed his cell wishing he had asked her out for dinner tonight, but that thought was brought to a halt by a sharp poke in ribs from Chubbs Gonzales.

Thirty-Eight

Jean-Louis Bernard felt ridiculous dressed in short beach pants, a Marcel T-shirt, bug-eyed sunglasses and a fanny pack. He was Parisian for Christ's sake. He would never wear such an outfit. Pete Shaw was dressed to match and looked even more uncomfortable. But they needed to be tourists at the height of summer to follow Gus Happy unnoticed.

When Gus finally left the hotel it was around eleven thirty. He walked down Rue Notre Dame and made a right at Place Toselli heading for a municipal rent-a-bike rack. He bent down to read the instructions but they were naturally in French. A waiter from the bistro in front of the bike rack came to help Gus get going. After entering a credit card and punching a few numbers Gus would soon be on his way down Rue Lepante heading for Place Massena and the sea. He adjusted the seat on the bike then paused at the bistro to have a coffee before he headed out.

Jean-Louis and Pete made a quick decision and retrieved their car a block away rather than following him on matching bikes. Their timing was good. When Pete arrived Gus was just setting off on his ride.

The streets in central Nice that Friday afternoon were packed with shoppers and double parked cars left unattended. The current philosophy in France is to park your car wherever you like and to hell with everyone. The narrow streets add to the frustration as well as the dozens of motor scooters which weave in and out of traffic like angry packs of bees.

Gus was making it easy for the two agents. He biked at a leisurely pace and came to rest at a small bistro on the edge of the gardens two blocks from the sea. He grabbed a newspaper and a pack of smokes from the shop next door and settled in at a table on the terrace for a bite to eat.

Jean-Louis and Pete found a parking spot and sat on a park bench opposite the bistro. They had their iPhones set for photos in case they needed to document their endeavors. Thirty minutes passed and Pete was getting hungry. He was about to get up to go across the street to grab two sandwiches when an elderly couple approached Gus and began to speak with him. Shaw held up his iPhone and zoomed into the faces taking multiple shots.

The look on Gus's face was surprise accompanied by shock as the couple spoke with him for about five minutes. They eventually moved casually down the street arm in arm. Gus sat quietly for a few moments then whipped out his cell phone and punched in a number.

Pete Shaw had already sent the photos from his phone to the FBI data bank. He thought to himself how much easier it was to get the bad guys today than it was twenty years ago.

There was only one problem: the bad guys had the same technology.

Thirty-Nine

Chubbs couldn't contain his excitement when the results of his web search on Alistair Krupp began to pour in. Chris was massaging his rib cage.

"Get a load of this chief, the search engine came up with a match on the name, born in London in 1959 by an Italian mother and a German father — and get this, the mother's maiden name was Vincezio-Paganini. That would put our assassin right in the picture if he does happen to be this Krupp guy."

Chris was beginning to see daylight. "…Anything else?'

Chubbs sighed. "Okay, we've got some weirdness here. The Alistair Krupp we have on line appears to have died at the age of nineteen in an auto accident outside of London in a town called Stevenage. The death certificate was issued by the coroner of said village on March 19, 1979."

Tension was overriding Chris's usually calm nature. "What the fuck is going on here?"

"Hold on amigo," Chubbs asserted, "with the current info we have on Alistair Krupp, this whole death thing could be a fake.

We've got a pretty good idea that this guy is around today. We just have to discover a reason for his mock death in '79."

Chris mused. "We not only need to know why, but how a kid of nineteen could pull this off?"

Chubbs rubbed the back of his neck. "Maybe he had friends in high places who were training him for his future career as an international hit man?"

Chris released the tension in his body and leaned back on the slats of the blue chair. "Jesus," he thought out loud, "has Alistair Krupp been a hired gun since he was twenty years old?"

Fatigue had set in big time. All Chris could think about was dinner with Ariel.

Forty

The Negresco is the last of the luxurious hotels built in the nineteenth century along the Promenade des Anglais facing the Mediterranean in Nice. It is still operative today. In its heyday, all of the finery which graces the interior of this exotic structure was appreciated by Royalty, impresarios, artists and the many characters which formed their unique societies. Whether they were cultured elitists or uncultured, well endowed barbarians, they all had one thing in common: the ability to lead an opulent lifestyle with all of its rewards.

Jonathan and Emily Parker occupied a suite on the third floor of the hotel which faced the sea. Cut flowers were brought in twice daily and a grand piano adorned their sitting room. Today, the traffic below overshadowed the sound of the sea lapping against the shore. Jonathan lay motionless on his bed recalling from an earlier epoch the sound of horse hooves clattering on the street and the grinding wheels of the carriages they drew.

He was meditating and at the same time assessing the damage

that he and his beloved were going through physically. With his eyes closed he released all the tension in his body, concentrating from the tips of his toes to the crown of his head: from Malkuth to Kether. His capacity to view the interior of his body was a skill earned centuries ago. His inner-perception could feel his blood circulating along the path of his spinal chakras. He commenced ancient breathing exercises which had the potential power to temporarily rejuvenate his body.

As he drifted into a trance he began to sift through the corridors of memory. Jonathan fast-tracked through all of the sages, saints and sinners that had touched his many lives: so many of them had altered the face of the planet forever. The world was no longer a place where gods walked with man.

Jonathan recalled the changes that overtook the collective psyche when electricity replaced the candle and the gas lamp. How mankind began to think smaller and smaller as life became easier, more convenient and less and less attached to Nature and the patterns of rural existence.

The evolution from villages and townships to cities and the metropolis: steel and cement environments where millions of people who have little or no compassion for others are crammed into buildings devoid of soul. Lifeless structures stacked one to the next unable to breathe. Living in boxes where the minimal psychic connection to an interior life is unavailable, while staring endlessly into a blue screen night after night with nothing to say.

The birth of the Industrial Revolution, mass production, transportation — computers — cyber space: when Jonathan experienced his first sighting of a steam engine racing through the Yorkshire countryside in the early nineteenth century, the minute he heard its roar and observed steam pouring out of the lungs of mashing metal he knew all would be "…Changed, changed utterly," as a friend in Jonathan's future, W.B. Yeats would declare in his poetry.

An unexpected pain began in Jonathan's shoulders. It took the majority of his psychic energy to overcome the sensation and return to his steady trance-like state. It was imperative to get their hands on the documents sealed into the lining of Paganini's violin box.

The contact with Gus Happy today at the bistro was the beginning of the final distillation of their needs. Jonathan had great confidence in Maria Sanoni's powers over the opposite sex. The fact that she appeared to really be in love was the crystallizing element required to realize their goals.

Jonathan thought about Emily. She was his main concern. Her breathing was becoming erratic. He loved her so much and could not imagine existence without her.

If the magic ritual that the Devil left behind is truly the document Jonathan believed it to be, then an extended period of life might be possible for he and his beloved.

The man who had lived for centuries stared at the ceiling, admiring the beautifully carved rosette that surrounded a glistening crystal chandelier. He recited an ancient prayer for strength and guidance and eventually fell asleep.

Forty-One

After the Parkers left Gus at the bistro, Gus called Maria in a panic and told her to meet him at their hotel right now. Maria had just stepped out of the shower. A million disoriented thoughts chased through her mind. Why were the Parkers here and how did they know about her and Gus?

She heard rapid footsteps coming down the corridor. Gus threw open the door and pounced onto the bed covering his eyes with his hands. "Jesus, the crap keeps getting bigger and bigger." He grappled for a cigarette, not noticing that Maria had already lit two. "Who in the fuck are Mr. and Mrs. Parker, and how do they know about us, the violin and the god damn killer on top of it?"

Maria sat down. "How and where did you run into them?" Her foot opened the room's mini bar and she grabbed a three ounce bottle of Smirnoff's.

Gus gave her a where-in-the-hell-is-mine look but answered her question. "Okay…here's what happened. I took one of those blue bikes for a cruise just like you told me to do. I found a small bistro grabbed a paper and some smokes to have a bite. God knows I deserve a fucking break from this horse shit."

Maria looked at him as if she were about to scold a child. Gus relented. "Okay, I'll watch the language. It's just that these two old geezers really took me by surprise." Gus butted out his cigarette. "Mr. Parker gave me a message for you."

Maria began to focus. "Tell me exactly what he told you, I mean *every* word."

Gus stared up at the ceiling in thought. "He told me to tell you that he was glad that you'd found happiness in Mr. Happy. At first I thought it was some kind of a joke but then his eyes bore into me like a drill motor and he said to tell the daughter of my soul that the time to strike is tomorrow."

Maria listened intently. "…Anything else?"

Gus now looked at Maria. "Yeah, he said to do it about two a.m. and that you shouldn't worry about the killer they'll take care of him." Gus had a lot of questions. "Excuse me, but who in the hell are these people and why do we need their help to break into a fucking art studio on a side street in the middle of a beach town."

Maria appeared to be thinking things over but didn't speak. Gus continued. "And so is this killer the one who did in Como? Is this violin so damn important that everyone involved has a chance of having their asses eliminated, including you and yours truly?" Maria went to the bed and wrapped her arms around Gus. He remained stiff. Gus, full of pessimism, was reverting back to his former self.

Maria stood up and began pacing around the room. She started in with no preliminaries. "Jonathan works for Max. I know very little about his wife except that they have been together for a very long time. He was my violin teacher in Paris many years ago."

Gus shot a quick upward glance at her.

"No, we were not lovers. He tried to help me become a

great musician. It wasn't meant to be. He gave me a book which changed my life. I became a good thief just like you Gus."

An eerie silence pervaded the atmosphere. It was as if Gus and Maria were in separate rooms. For Gus, right now, all that mattered was business. It was time to wrap this bird! His keen sense of concentration was returning to his face. Maria had given him all the information he needed to pull this job off solo. Better that way.

It was Friday, September the eleventh, 2009 and by Sunday morning he was sure he'd be the hell out of France — mission accomplished.

Forty-Two

Chris stood on the balcony of his hotel room with a half-empty bottle of Heineken in his hand. He was trying to enjoy the last vestiges of the sun before it disappeared over the roof.

Five o'clock arrived with a knock at his door. After the group settled in, Chris asked Chubbs to update the other agents on Alistair Krupp, and the Parkers. Chris told his co-workers about the message left at the embassy and the disappearing act perpetrated by the assassin at the age of twenty.

Ariel was the first to speak. "No wonder this guy has been untraceable. If Krupp is the one who took out Como in Italy then I'd say that our "man in black" must be a lot closer than we think."

Chris posited. "I'll bet the son of a bitch is staying in this hotel he's so close!" Chris grabbed another beer, inviting the others to do the same.

"Jonathan and Emily Parker have just arrived on the scene. Pete and Jean-Louis caught them meeting up with Gus Happy this morning. Chubbs tracked them down and low and behold, they're two blocks away registered at the hotel Negresco. I've asked the Municipal police to pick them up and bring them here for questioning. I'm not sure what piece of the puzzle they represent but we're damn well going to find out."

Pete Shaw broke in. "What's our excuse for rounding them up?"

Chris finished a swig of beer. "Well, they're American tourists abroad and we're concerned for their safety. That's a good enough excuse even if they're smart enough to know it's a ploy."

Chris's cell went off. The local police were on their way upstairs with the Parkers. There was a knock at the door. Chris opened it to meet two uniformed policemen and a smartly dressed elderly couple.

"Who in the hell are you two?" Chris shot out.

The man who closely resembled Jonathan Parker shifted nervously on his feet. He spoke with a British accent. "Me and the Mrs. weren't doing any harm, honest. I don't know what this is all about, but believe us, we was just doing an American bloke a favor, that's all, just a little favor."

Chris told the couple to sit down. "How did this favor come about?"

The Englishman's forehead was drenched in sweat. "You see, we came down from Brighton for the holidays. We was mindin' our own business, taking a little walk along the promenade when this American chap and his wife came up and introduced themselves."

Chris interrupted. "…And you are?"

"Oh right, we are the Harveys, Gerald and Beryl. The couple that approached us called themselves Mr. and Mrs. Alistair Krupp. "

Chubbs looked at Chris with wide grin. "Wow, this guy Parker is quite a comedian."

Chris replied, "Yeah, and he's getting funnier every minute."

Gerald Harvey then proceeded to tell the agents the details. It seems that the man calling himself Alistair Krupp was a big

Hollywood producer and wanted to avoid the local media by hiring the Harveys to pose in their place for a few hours while they relocated to another hotel. The couple offered the Harveys two hundred Euros and told them to spend the night if they wished and order up room service free of charge.

After a few more questions the Harveys signed a written statement and were released. The room became quiet and pensive. Chris looked over at Agent Bernard.

"Jean-Louis, you said earlier today that Gus Happy and Maria stopped by the Hotel de Ville to examine some documents before their scheduled appointment with the real estate agent. Is that correct?"

"Oui Monsieur Clarke. I checked with the clerk at the office after the couple left. They had requested to examine the architectural changes over the past seventy years to the building they were going to visit."

Chris straightened up. "What did they find out?"

The French agent cleared his throat. "Indeed there were changes. A famous Italian sculptor living in Nice in the nineteen fifties purchased the old apartment of Paganini's and the one directly beneath it. He obtained permission to tear out the floor of Paganini's apartment to make room for his larger works. When the artist passed away in 1976, his widow sold the complex back to the city which then returned the interior structure to its original setting."

Although his room was a non-smoking area Chris lit up. "Did you get the name of this sculptor?"

Oui Monsieur, bien sur…his name was Antonius Petrarchus. Many of his works are featured in the gardens all over Nice."

Chris pivoted to Ariel. "Wasn't Petrarchus the name of the gallery you followed Maria to?"

Ariel nodded her head. "Yes, but it is Niccolo Petrarchus. I checked up. He's the the son of Antonius."

Chris stood up abruptly and clapped his hands together

like a sports coach signaling a victory. "Ladies and gentlemen, I believe that we now know where the Devil's violin has been hiding for the past sixty years or so. Antonius Petrarchus must have discovered it beneath the flooring of Paganini's apartment while the modifications were taking place. He probably figured out pretty quickly what the treasure was and was smart enough to tuck it away for the future." Chris took another beer. "Why Paganini stashed the fiddle beneath the flooring is anyone's guess."

Pete Shaw spoke up. "Reminds me of a case we had down south a few years back. There was a fellow who robbed a bank and got away with around a million dollars. We never did catch him and wouldn't have known a damn thing about it except that the house he lived in was sold after he died and the new owners found several hundred thousand dollars behind a false wall in the den. There was a letter tucked into one of the bags addressed to his son that never got posted. Maybe this here Paganini fellow had the same problem. He probably forgot to, or died before he had the time to tell his next of kin about the stash."

Chris smiled at Pete. "I think your take is about as close as we're going to get to the truth. I want a twenty-four hour surveillance on the art studio starting immediately. We'll request that the locals have police in the area for the rest of the day and tonight after the gallery closes, Agent George and I will take the first shift at eight o'clock. Jean-Louis, you and Pete relieve us at one a.m. and stay until sunrise. Chubbs, I'd like you to stay in touch with the Bureau search engine and continue to gather info on our players." Chris tossed his empty beer in the trash can. "My gut feeling tells me that the violin is in the studio and has been hidden by the son of Antonius Petrarchus for nearly fifty years."

Chris faced the group to wrap things up. "Our 'man in black,' the Parkers, along with Gus Happy and Maria Sanoni will more than likely make their moves in the next forty eight hours. Let's stay on our toes and bring this case to a close without any bloodshed — particularly our own!"

The meeting adjourned and Chris requested that Ariel remain behind to make a plan for their evening stake out.

Forty-Three

Chris and Ariel agreed to share an early dinner before their surveillance shift at eight o'clock. Chris closed the door to his room full of anticipation and anxiety.

The current case took precedence but his unexpected feelings for Ariel were rallying hard for first place. It could not be a more inconvenient time to become smitten, let alone with a woman who was part of the Bureau. It was a strange attraction, for, though they had been in training together twenty years ago, Chris was happily married at the time and he had no idea about Ariel's love life. Besides, their focus was learning how to get the bad guys.

Chris changed into his black denim jeans with a Hugo Boss sand-colored sport jacket. The last thing he wanted to look like was a cop. He arrived at the bistro a little before their rendezvous and easily secured a table on the terrace: no self respecting European would think of dining this early.

Chris suddenly realized that he was by himself and alone with his thoughts for the first time in weeks. Minutes trudged by like hours. Although he and Brenda had broken up years ago, he was riddled with guilt about his urge for Ariel. The unexpected brush of a soft hand across his cheek pulled him out of his funk. They ordered drinks and tapas as their conversation began with the casual enthusiasm of a first date.

One lone diner in particular, just three tables away, admired the couple and thought they were a cute pair. He smoked his gold-tipped cigarillo languidly as he scanned the carte du jour through his gold-rimmed glasses deciding what delicacy would please him most this evening.

Forty-Four

Agents Clarke and George spent Friday night in an unmarked sedan staring at empty streets.

Chris was uncomfortable throughout the entire watch. They chatted while keeping an eye on the closed sculpture gallery, yet their body language hinted at more than what one should expect from two law enforcement officers on a stake-out.

Agents Shaw and Bernard tapped on the driver's window a few minutes before one a.m.. Chris updated them and then offered to walk Ariel back to her hotel two blocks away.

They strolled in silence. Finally, Chris couldn't stand it anymore. He stopped Ariel, facing her with his hands on her shoulders and found the courage to say what needed to be said. "Look, there's something I've got to say and now is as good a time as any." Chris felt relieved that he'd started his confession but he paused, not really knowing how to finish his thoughts.

Ariel, sporting a big smile, took the ball and ran with it. "You don't have to say a thing Chris. We're both adults and you wouldn't feel the way you do right now if I didn't feel that way too. I felt the sparks flying back at Quantico and they returned this morning at the embassy. I was married for a brief time to an attorney but, well, you know, the demands of two professionals under the same roof."

Ariel reached up and gave Chris a peck on the cheek that was full-lipped and withdrawn hesitantly. She smiled from ear to ear. "Let's close this case and see if we can't grab a little time together afterwards. Sound good, partner?"

Then it happened: an unexpected change in Ariel's facial expression as she peered over Chris's shoulder. He knew from experience what it meant but he reacted too late. Then he felt a blunt object pressing against his ribcage accompanied by a soft voice near his ear.

"My, my Agent Clarke you and Agent George make such a lovely couple. If you're smart and do as I tell you to, this evening will conclude peacefully enough and you'll be alive in the morning to enjoy each other's company for breakfast."

Chris wanted to make a move and knew that Ariel would be right there with him if he did, but there was something about the predator's voice that was unnerving. Chris relaxed his shoulders and the man spun him around to face the wall as he invited Ariel to do the same. The stranger removed their weapons and told them to not turn around until he said so.

Chris searched his mind trying to find a psychological advantage. "So, may I assume that we are having the pleasure of meeting Mr. Alistair Krupp?"

"You're a clever one Agent Clarke. But let's say that the pleasure will begin after the next thirty minutes or so have passed. Shall we return to Rue Niepce and proceed with the business at hand?" For Alistair finding the couple on the street alone was ideal. He would gather up the violin and take care of the two agents at the same time leaving no witnesses.

The trio began their march back along Rue de Paris. Chris could see the unmarked car with the two agents sitting upright in the front seats. He knew that it was just a matter of a few seconds before Pete and Jean-Louis would spot them and react. As Chris was contemplating his next move, the reptilian-like voice behind him spoke. "There's no reason to be hopeful of a dashing rescue by your brothers in arms. They are peacefully resting with a little help from an injection I carry with me for just such occasions. They should be in dreamland until the sun rises."

Chris focused his eyes on the windshield of the stake-out vehicle under the light of the yellow street lamp. Both agents Shaw and Bernard were sitting upright, perfectly still, oblivious to all around them: out cold.

Alistair Krupp guided the pair to the front door of the Petrarchus gallery then paused to remove an object from his coat pocket. It appeared to be a cell phone but there were only six buttons on the face of it. While focusing the muzzle of his hand gun on the two agents, his free hand punched a series of buttons and the front door made a clicking sound. Alistair told Chris to push the door open and to enter with Ariel. Ariel had said nothing up to this point. Training and experience had taught her that two voices asking questions or making demands of an aggressor might cause a moment of panic that could be life-threatening.

Chris took a stab at acquiring Ariel's freedom. "Look, Alistair, you don't need both of us around here to do what you want to do. We all know that you want your family's violin — you've already killed for it. So, let Agent George go and…"

Alistair gave Chris a crack on the head with the butt of his hand gun. Chris fell forward on his knees smacking the floor of the entrance. Ariel started to react but Alistair gave her such a menacing look that she froze in her tracks. Krupp was not your average bad guy. His eyes told you that inducing bodily harm was as natural to him as breathing.

As Chris was recovering, Alistair closed the door behind them. He told Chris and Ariel to sit on the floor, back to back with their legs straight in front of them. He then manipulated his little black box and shut down the entire alarm system.

It was now the time of discovery. Alistair had followed Gus and Maria since day one, leaving them alone in the mountain cabin because he knew where they were. He needed Maria to show him the way to his family treasure. Only a fire proof lead-lined door now stood between the distant relative of Paganini and the precious violin.

Chris was thinking about Chubbs. Where in the hell was he? If he was back at the hotel asleep, there would be very little chance of a burst-through-the-door-guns-ablazin' rescue.

The situation was looking bleak. The only hope was to make it through the next few minutes alive.

Forty-Five

The city of Nice has one of the most efficient sanitation departments in all of Europe. Rubbish is collected three times a day starting around eight thirty in the evening. As the trash trucks barrel through the narrow streets, the noise made by their garrulous operators as they collect, dump, and compact the trash is heard by everyone. The same procedure takes place around ten thirty and once more at one a.m.. The locals have adapted to these nightly intrusions and are rarely disturbed. However, most tourists find it difficult to get back to sleep after the early morning pickup.

Gus Happy awoke abruptly at a quarter past one in the darkness of their room trying to figure out if World War III had just begun on the street below his hotel window, or if someone had decided to demolish a building in the cooler air of the blackened night.

He reached for his cigarettes. When he flicked his lighter the flame caught the reclining body of Maria. Shadows danced along her torso. His lips formed a slight smile but it could not deaden the turbulent thoughts racing through his mind at the moment.

What if this Parker couple and the "man in black" were making their move tonight, Friday? Why did Maria decide to strike tomorrow night just because Jonathan Parker told her to do so?

Gus slung his legs off the side of the bed and dressed quietly. He knew where the Devil's violin was supposed to be in the art gallery and it shouldn't take more than thirty minutes to grab the booty and run. He gathered up the tools he would need and stuffed his Glock down the back of his trousers. He took the stairwell instead of the elevator and hit the street as the trash truck was pulling away. Even this late at night it was still around ninety degrees and his footsteps echoed off of the sidewalk as he headed out noticing that the musty smell in the air reminded him of sections of L.A.

As he approached the entrance to the gallery all seemed calm. He threw his cigarette butt into the street and leaned his head against the door to listen.

Forty-Six

As Alistair was manipulating the lock on the storage door he didn't notice the slight clicking sound coming from the entrance. Neither did Chris or Ariel.

It took less than a minute for Alistair to accomplish his goal. He turned the handle and pushed the door ajar. What he saw in the crack of the door jamb surprised him. There was a source of illumination coming from within. He raised his hand gun and slowly entered the room. There, sitting casually on a block of marble was Jonathan Parker with a pink cashmere sweater draped over his shoulders and a gutted violin case on the floor. Reposing perpendicular to his feet was the famed violin that Niccolo Paganini had built his legend upon. It seemed to vibrate as if it were capable of playing on its own. A set of parchment documents lay spread across Jonathan's lap. He had the same warm smile on his face as he did the day that Alistair met him in the park in Milan.

"You're early," Jonathan smiled, "I was expecting you in about thirty minutes." Jonathan leaped to his feet as if he were twenty years old. "Are our friends from the FBI comfortable? Cover me while I tape their arms together and perhaps a piece across the mouths just for precautions sake…eh?" Jonathan stepped over the violin and came through the storage door as he were about to fetch some ice cubes for a cocktail.

Alistair was shocked into submission. Jonathan secured the two agents and then turned to Alistair. "Well, my unwilling friend, here we are together again. I've taken the liberty of performing the task which you had reserved for yourself and I hope you're not offended. I've examined the instrument and I can assure you that this is your thrice-great grandfather's violin." Jonathan paused for a reaction from Alistair but the assassin remained quiet. "Oh by the way, I found what I was looking for: the documents maestro Paganini hid in the lining of the violin box."

As Jonathan was talking, Alistair was deciding whether or not to do away with all three of them right now and make a hasty retreat with the violin finally in his possession. Once again, his curiosity got the better of him. "Well Parker, I'm sure that you won't mind sharing with me the secrets contained in those documents my distant relative left behind? Was it true that he had developed a method explaining the system behind his incredible technique?"

Jonathan let out a slight laugh holding his hand over his mouth to soften the sound. "Bravo Alistair, you're up on your family history. It's a short document and I'd be happy to read it to you." Jonathan stepped back into the storage room and sat on the marble block. "There are three documents here. One in Latin from the sixteenth century, followed by an Italian translation dated 1756. The one I will read to you is in English and is dated 1810. It is my belief that Paganini commissioned it while touring in England at that time. We shall never know why he desired a copy in English, but it is very much to our advantage at this moment."

"Well, here we are then." Jonathan shuffled the documents until the English version was on top.

Michael on high before Nine families of Angels knowing the wrath and forgiveness He discloses.

The first in the Garden separated the Tree from its branches, yet, there were discarded twigs that formed a mightier Tree.

To rest beneath the shade of this Tree is considered a sin. When the North wind blows we gather beneath its bows to escape idleness, moving along the green line that encircles us all.

From the third light to the fourth day we enter the Night of the body. In six days cedars came forth out of Lebanon and Paradise was found to be in the center and not at the top.

And from this place a River flows dividing into many streams. If we do not seek His benevolence then all things dependeth on Fate.

Animated and jubilant, we rush the gates knowing the rainy season clings to the South where the Unicorn grazes relentlessly. Daemon est Deus inversus – The Devil is God upside down.

Two chariots fall from the Tree. One with wheels, the other sprouts wings which ascendeth Heavenward.

In infinite wisdom He created the elements and made us spring forth from the Waters of Life.

No Angel with six wings has ever been transformed for balance does not allow change.

Odd numbers soothe broken souls.

Clothed in our garment of existence, we Love Fear and Fear Love.

The House of Judgment is righteous bringing prophecy until the Spirit ceases to desire.

We listen to the voice of the Daughter of the King which humbles the Hosts of Heaven— Counting backwards from Ten.

Amen

Jonathan finished and looked up at Alistair with his hands folded in his lap. The look on Alistair's face was both menacing and questioning. The two men stared each other down for a few moments then Alistair spoke. "So what is the gibberish all about? Surely you didn't travel half way around the globe, risking your life, just to retrieve a paper filled with such nonsense?"

Jonathan waved him off. "I'll grant you this, Alistair. To the uninitiated it can serve no purpose. But your time-honored relative and many others including yours truly are associated with a tradition that pre-dates the Christian era. People are only now beginning to suspect and to unravel the intricate web of this movement and the role that it has played in shaping the destiny of mankind. Without this society and its far-reaching concepts which touch upon all races, religions, and cultures there would have been no evolution in the sciences, and the arts. The progress of man's intellectual development would never have reached the creative and analytical heights of our current age." Jonathan glanced around the room as if her were looking for something.

Alistair was growing impatient. "Well old man, I don't hear one word within this bullshit that talks about Paganini's violin technique. Can you explain that away?"

Jonathan resumed his warm smile. "On the surface you're correct in your observation, but in fact this document is directly related to his capacity to invent, or should I say imagine, his concept of playing the violin which changed the entire violin world overnight. This ancient text is a formula for strengthening the imaginative faculties as well as extending the capacity of physical life itself. It is extremely valuable in the proper hands: completely useless to the uninformed."

Krupp was finished with Parker's philosophical clap-trap. He had no more time to debate the fate of the three persons before him. He decided to do away with them.

Suddenly, the front door of the gallery flew open with an

explosive sound. The body of Gus Happy vaulted across the floor sliding face down followed by Chubbs Gonzales wielding his weapon grasped between both hands, pointing it at Alistair and yelling at the top of his lungs, "Put the weapon down…right now…I mean now god-damnit or you're fucking toast!"

Chris had twisted his neck to observe the excitement and realized two things immediately. One, that Chubbs looked as big as the Amazing Hulk and two, that he had never heard Chubbs curse in the ten years they had been partners.

Alistair wheeled around and got off a shot in Chubb's direction which grazed his shoulder. At the same time Chubbs let off three rounds which hit Alistair in the chest and stomach. "The man in black" folded like a rag doll and hit the floor without another sound.

Breathing hard, Chubbs screamed, "Hey partners, you okay?" He moved towards Chris and Ariel while focusing the gun on Jonathan Parker. Gus was face down and seemed to be out cold.

With his adrenaline flowing, Chubbs ripped off the duct tape from Chris and Ariel's mouths.

"Yow-itch!!" Chris yelled, "Christ, you big lug, what in the hell took you so long?" Ariel was spitting out particles of tape.

Chubbs bent down to release their arms and the two agents stood up. Chubbs ordered Jonathan Parker to come out of the storage room and sit on the floor next to Gus Happy.

"Well chief, it's like this. I got a call from Pete Shaw asking me to run down to McDonald's and bring them some burgers and cokes. Those dumbbells had forgotten to pack a snack for their all-nighter."

Ariel had quickly regained her composure and retrieved both their weapons from the body of Alistair Krupp as well as bagging his hand gun.

Chubbs continued with a Cheshire-cat grin on his face. "You know me and McDonald's buddy, that was a no-prob to do them that favor. When I arrived, I knocked on the car window with no response. Then I looked over at the gallery and spotted Gus Happy with his head against the door. I cupped my hands against the driver's side window and could see that Pete and Jean-Louis were still breathing so I headed over here to crash the party."

Chris took charge, pleased that Ariel had already called the local police and medical support for Pete, Jean-Louis and Chubbs's shoulder wound. Chris ordered Chubbs to go with her to have his wound looked at and to assist with the two drugged agents.

Without saying a word, Chris handcuffed Jonathan Parker and examined the lifeless body of Alistair Krupp, alias "the man in black." Thinking that the crime scene was secure, Chris called FBI Bureau headquarters back in Washington D.C. to update them on the situation.

Forty-Seven

A voice echoed off the cement walls of the dimly lit gallery as if it were coming from the lips of an apparition. It was soft and flowing although the words somehow didn't match the ethereal quality. For a brief moment, Chris thought he was hallucinating.

"Dear, you shouldn't sit on your sweater in this god awful filthy place. It's one hundred percent Alpaca cashmere. And now officer, will you please turn over your weapon and remove the handcuffs from my husband's wrists. He's a rather talented violinist and I doubt the lack of circulation to his hands is beneficial."

Chris recognized the voice immediately; the woman on the embassy's voice mail. She must have been hiding the whole time in a dark corner of the storage room. Neither agent had thought to search the premises after the shooting. Caught up in the moment they had completely forgotten about Emily Parker. She was aiming an AK-47 at Chris as casually as if it were a Chanel hand bag. Chris bent down and uncuffed his prisoner. Jonathan shook the dust off of his sweater while beaming proudly at his wife.

Chris knew that Ariel and Chubbs would return in a matter of seconds: he needed a plan.

Just then, Chris heard a noise as if a frightened cat were scurrying away. Before he could check the source, he saw Emily Parker flying through the air. Gus Happy had suddenly come back to life and had swept his legs across the floor catching the woman off guard behind her knees. Her weapon flew out of her hands and slammed into the wall. Gus quickly jumped to his feet brandishing his Glock and ordered the Parkers and Chris Clarke to stay put.

Chris tried to appeal to Gus's sensibility. "Gus, officially we have nothing on you, you haven't committed a crime that we're aware of. Planning a robbery is not an offence unless you do it. If you hand over your weapon to me right now, I will credit you with assisting the authorities in closing this case. If you don't surrender, I'll have to consider you one of them." Chris arched his head in the direction of the Parkers.

Gus herded Chris and the Parkers into the storage room. He spoke for the first time since his arrival. "Nice chatting with you — I'm outta here." With that, he scooped up the Devil's violin, backed out of the vault and locked the door. True to form, Gus grabbed and ran. No one noticed the slippery sneak thief running down Rue Niepce as the local authorities were focused on the agents receiving medical care. He speed dialed Maria with his free hand and told the sleeping princess to meet him down stairs a.s.a.p. They were out of here with the prize.

Shortly after Gus made his escape with the violin, Ariel George returned and realized what had happened. She unlocked the storage door and made sure that Chris had the Parkers secured, then she dashed out and ran down the block in pursuit of Gus. She returned in ten minutes, empty handed. There was no sign of the couple, in their room or on the streets. They had fled the scene by means unknown. Ariel sent out an APB to local authorities to be on the lookout for the couple, who by now could be anywhere.

Chris left Ariel in charge of the Parkers and went over to check on the status of Jean-Louis, Pete, and Chubbs. Gonzales had his right shoulder bandaged up from the gunshot wound but seemed no worse for the wear. Shaw and Bernard were coming out of the fog, slowly but surely. Chris updated the crew on Gus Happy's quick exit, admitting that the violin appeared to be a goner.

Chubbs was trying to put his coat on over his shoulder. "Well chief, at least we got our man."

Chris helped Chubbs. "Thanks to you amigo the rest of us are still breathing. You've earned a well deserved commendation on this one. You okay?"

Chubbs nodded while breathing hard. "I only did what I've been trained to do, partner. But I still don't get how the Parkers fit into all of this? What was so important about those documents hidden in the violin case?"

Chris lit a cigarette. "While I was a temporary prisoner I listened to Parker reading and explaining the document to Alistair. It appears to be an ancient ritual that some secret society has treasured for centuries: some mumbo-jumbo about the imagination and the possibility of extending life beyond the normal span. It could be a code of some kind. We'll know more when our experts take a crack at it."

Chris's cell phone went off and he stepped away from the crowd to hear the caller. Chubbs could just hear Chris's response to the call. "Yes sir...right, yes sir, of course...but...yes sir, I understand, will do. Is there anything else I should know? Right...yes sir, I'll inform the other agents. Thank you sir, good night."

Chris slowly folded his cell phone and looked up at the sky. Chubbs meandered over towards Chris and put his good arm on his boss's shoulder. "What's up chief?"

"Well I thought I'd heard it all." Chris continued to look at the heavens. "That was FBI Director Halligan's top aid calling from D.C.. There's a big well done for all involved in the termination of Alistair Krupp. However, we have strict orders to release the Parkers with the set of documents in their possession."

Chubbs released his arm from Chris's shoulder. "I don't get it. These people are armed and dangerous. What gives?"

Chris continued to stare off into space. "I'm not sure how much influence the Parkers have but one thing I know for sure is that by direct orders of Director Halligan, these folks are *hands off*, and that's that."

Chris turned to Chubbs. "Have they located Niccolo Petrarchus yet?"

"Sure have, chief. He started babbling to the police something about the ghost of Paganini, but who in hell knows what that's all about?"

Chris stared off. "We may never know, bud."

Forty-Eight

By three in the morning the gallery was mobbed with law enforcement officials and local media. Forensic and medical teams were scouring the crime scene and preparing to remove Alistair Krupp's remains. Sleepy-eyed newspaper and TV journalists were arriving in vans giving the neighborhood a carnival atmosphere.

The Parkers were seated in the storage room on two separate blocks of marble. Jonathan and Emily looked like they'd been through nothing more than dinner and a show. They were totally relaxed and amazingly tidy under the circumstances.

Chris knelt down in front of them to be at their eye level. He gazed silently at each of their faces, addressing Emily first. "That was you that called the embassy and left the message revealing the identity of the "man in black" — am I right?"

Emily Parker answered in a soft voice. "Yes it was. I considered it my duty to inform the authorities of such a dangerous criminal. The disguised voice was an attempt to remain anonymous."

Chris stared at her for a few moments. "I don't suppose that you'd be willing to tell the Department just how you knew that we were looking for such a person? And also, I'd like you to reveal your sources. Quite frankly, the Bureau has been chasing down this killer for over a decade and with all of the technology available to us we haven't even come close to your findings."

Jonathan Parker cut in before Emily could answer. "Agent Clarke, you are making the false assumption that the resources of the Federal Bureau of Investigation and the United States Government are all inclusive. You assume that no morsel of information could be out of your grasp with all of the data banks you command." Jonathan offered Chris a fatherly smile. "I assure you, right here and now, that there are other means of fact gathering that have absolutely no relationship to, or with, the world of cyber space. Methods of acquiring knowledge that are centuries old. As to why we are involved with this predicament, I'm afraid that shall have to remain a secret for the time being." Jonathan Parker reached down to brush a particle of marble dust from his sweater as if there was nothing left to do.

Chris was angry but he had his orders. "So, you two consider yourselves to be a couple of upstanding citizens who just happen to get caught in the middle of an FBI investigation and felt compelled to do your part for God and Country?"

Jonathan beamed. "I couldn't have put it better myself."

"And I suppose that toting around an AK-47 in your luggage is standard travel for senior jet setters like yourselves?"

The Parkers looked at each other and burst out laughing. Emily spoke. "Dear me, have you examined the weapon? It's a plastic toy. We purchased it in the neighborhood today thinking we might need it to scare off poor Alistair."

Chris rose to his feet to retrieve the item from the corner of the gallery. He realized the minute he got close to it that it was a fake. In the dark he couldn't tell. He picked it up and handed it to one of the forensic workers to have it bagged as evidence. Chris went back to face the Parkers. "I have been informed in the past few minutes by our Bureau Chief in Washington to let both of you go. You are not to be charged and the documents you discovered tonight are to leave with you." Chris paused to light a cigarette. "I can't begin to tell you how much this pisses me off." He blew the smoke off towards the Parkers. He waited for a response of some kind but none was offered. "Just who in the hell are you two?"

Jonathan stood up while assisting his wife to do the same. Chris noticed his eyes for the first time. They seemed to be lit from within.

"That is an excellent question young man. It is a curiosity which has captivated the great minds of humanity since the beginning of time. Just who are we, and where are we going, and for that matter, where did we come from?"

Clarke and Parker locked eyes for a few seconds then Jonathan turned away to gather up the documents as if preparing to leave, which was very much his intent.

Unnoticed, a black Mercedes had quietly inched its way along Rue Niepce and had stopped opposite the gallery.

Jonathan asked Chris very politely if they were free to go. Chris escorted the couple to the door and waved them through as if he were addressing royalty.

As they headed towards the limo, the passenger door flew open and out stepped Donald Sheldon. He saluted Chris while opening the rear door for the Parkers. Within seconds, the vehicle moved down the street into the still darkness, turned right on Rue Notre Dame and vanished.

Forty-Nine

The Air Bus 360 took off smoothly from Milan International Airport on Sunday morning, September 13, 2009, with two hundred and seventy passengers bound for Montreal, Canada. Included on the passenger list were Mr. and Mrs. Ralph Hampton, Canadian citizens, who were returning to their homeland after a three week vacation abroad.

Ralph was not particularly fond of air travel. He told his wife in no uncertain terms that this was to be their last voyage abroad. Carol Hampton just smiled at her boyish looking forty year old husband and gave him a peck on the cheek to calm him down. In the short time they'd been married, Carol had learned how to navigate smoothly through her husband's moods. His attention was now taken by the window seat view of the landscape below, fading away as they ascended through light clouds.

At the same time, Carol opened up her hand bag and removed a small pocket mirror. She held it at arm's length, moving her head back and forth to admire her new hair color. She never thought in her thirty five years of living as a brunette that she would ever be a blonde. Her olive complexion made it seem unfeasible. But here she was, blonde and loving it!

Ralph had been grumpy ever since he had his head shaved to a completely bald and polished state. Carol thought he looked cute, especially with his newly pierced diamond stud earring in his left ear. Ralph missed his blonde curls. They were part of him: a grand portion of his self image.

Both Ralph and Carol knew that their hair or the lack of it didn't have any relevance to the "big picture." After what they'd been through in the past few weeks they were safely on their way home.

Montreal has always been considered the best combination of Europe and America. A profusion of art galleries frequented by a literate population, along with world class restaurants wedged between trendy boutiques, alongside Home Depot, professional sports, and burger joints featuring great chocolate shakes; the best of both worlds for a couple born on separate continents.

The plane had been in the air for over an hour without a word being spoken. Finally, Ralph turned away from the window and glanced over at Carol, who was leafing through a copy of Vogue magazine.

He moved his lips close to Carol's ear and whispered. "I can't stand the fucking name 'Ralph', and you look about as much like a 'Carol' as," Gus smiled, "…Sophia Loren."

Maria let out one of her patented giggles and gave Gus a big hug. "It is how you say, time for us to 'hang in there' and 'count our lucky moons' — correct?"

Gus let out a short laugh. "Lucky stars babe, lucky stars."

CHAPTER FIFTY

The four agents involved in the case were gathered in the lobby of the Meridien Hotel awaiting a series of cabs to take them to their flights departing Nice International this Monday morning.

It had been a whirlwind operation beginning with their first meeting at the US embassy early Friday morning and the culmination of their activities at the crime scene in the sculpture gallery early Saturday morning. It took most of the remaining weekend to file reports and wrap up details. Every face expressed fatigue.

Agent Pete Shaw was being summoned back to Nashville for a debriefing of the events. He reclined in a leather lobby chair, eyes closed, chewing on a toothpick.

French Intelligence agent Jean-Louis Bernard was on his cell phone talking rapidly to his wife in Paris. He seemed oblivious to those around him and his voice was loud and intense.

Chubbs Gonzales seemed content to be observing his partner and Ariel George holding hands, talking softly to one another.

Chris Clarke stood up, having a sudden urge to address the

group. "Agents George, Bernard and Shaw, I'd like to take…" Suddenly he realized what he'd said. Their last names in that order spelled out the name of the famous literary icon. The group hesitated for a moment and then burst out laughing. Jean-Louis joined in not sure what was so funny. Chris continued.

"Jesus Christ. Well listen up folks. In a few minutes we'll be heading our separate ways and I just wanted to say thanks for all of your help. We made a great team and even though we missed out on the violin, we got the bad guy. The Department still needs to find the individual responsible for ordering the copy of the fiddle in the first place and I'm not stopping until I find out who in the hell the Parkers are and why they mean so much to the U.S. government." Chris lit a cigarette. "Gus Happy and Maria seemed to have just vanished into thin air. There's still a lot of unanswered questions and I…" Ariel grabbed Chris's arm. "Hey chief, the cabs are pulling up, it's time to go."

Several taxi drivers entered the lobby of the Meridien searching for their fares: just another day in the life of shuttling persons to and fro.

Fifty-One

On Monday morning, October 19, 2009, the Los Angeles basin was blessed with the cleanest air it had experienced in weeks. A steady light drizzle which had started the day before was a major contributor.

That overcast morning Max Pendleton was standing in his front garden dressed in pale green corduroy slacks, a black pull-over jersey, while his head was protected from the slight mist by a white Panama hat. He was surveying his plants while his wife was gathering a bunch of dew-soaked roses for their breakfast table. Max was appreciating his lifetime of accomplishments and the rewards his hard work had produced.

He was about to head back indoors when the bell at the garden gate rang. It was the postman George, smiling while waving a small parcel over his head. Max casually bounded down the brick stairs to greet him.

"My, my Mr. Pendleton your garden sure is radiant after last night's rain. I do believe that yours is the best in neighborhood." For a few seconds both men glanced at the multicolored expanse.

George broke the silence. "This here package comes all the way from Canada. I'll need you to sign for it."

Max put the light, oblong parcel under his arm, signed on the dotted line, wished George a good day and headed back up the stairs.

As he passed his wife on the way he told her he'd be in his office for a while. She waved at him, blowing a kiss then turned back to her rose garden wondering if she shouldn't pick a few more; they were so beautiful this morning.

Fifty-Two

San Diego FBI Bureau Chief Ted Gerard's office was typical of any one of high ranking governmental prestige: it was thoroughly intimidating.

It featured a massive mahogany desk, mounted with a state-of-the-arts computer, surrounded by tons of colored folders, one stacked upon the other, case after case load. On the wall behind Ted's desk were various framed photos with dignitaries. The space to the left of his over-sized leather desk chair boasted a shot of Ted Gerard shaking hands with Bill Clinton. Next to this unique moment of intimacy is a photo of Ted embracing George W. Bush senior. Centered above these two photos is another portrait of the Bureau Chief with President Barack Obama: all bases covered.

The largest photo on display however, is a beaming Gerard, "Ping" driver in hand, flanked on either side by Arnold Palmer and Jack Nicklaus. Away from the Bureau's responsibilities, Ted lived for golf.

To the left side of his desk sat an oak bookcase. The double doors are inset with glass for viewing. The carved oak piece of furniture would be ideal for a rare book collection. Ted replaced the shelves with racks. A dozen high caliber rifles were proudly displayed with NRA stickers prominently affixed to both glass panels.

Framed letters and documents of commendation also adorned the office space. One curious photo off to the side showed Gerard in camouflaged fatigues surrounded by soldiers in Vietnam. The photo was dated 1965. He looked about thirty five years old. No one at the Bureau had any idea as to Ted's real age. His retirement was announced five years ago, but here he sat, reviewing a current case file preparing for his meeting this Monday morning with Agents Clarke and Gonzales.

There was a knock at the door. Chief Gerard barked out "enter" and Chris and Chubbs sat down in front of his desk. Directly in front of Ted was a huge white marble ashtray. Although smoking was prohibited in all Federal buildings he puffed away on a black cigar. His eyes never left the report he as he began to speak. "Well boys, how was your vacation in Europe?"

Chris cleared his throat. He and Gerard had butted heads before. "As a matter of fact chief, there wasn't a lot of time to hit the tourist spots." Chris truly despised Gerard's sarcasm. "As the report you have before you indicates, the "man in black," thanks mostly to Agent Gonzales, is history."

Ted gazed up at Chubbs for a brief moment looking over the rims of his half-moon reading glasses. "Good job Gonzales." Coming from Ted Gerard, this casual compliment was equal to something on the level of "thanks for saving the world".

Chubbs acknowledged Ted's remark with a nod of his head.

Ted removed his glasses and threw them at the table top. He rubbed his eyes and pushed himself back into his chair. He gave both agents a stern look. "I see in your report that we still have some unanswered questions." The Bureau chief flipped through a few pages. "For instance, have either of you any idea what happened to the violin? And do we know if the one the thieves got away with is the real McCoy or a copy?"

Chris was attempting to control his Irish temper. "The violin, as far as we know sir, was last known to be cradled in the arms of Gustav Edward Happy as he was scurrying down Rue Niepce. I imagine that if we need to know the current location of said item we could just ring up your friends the Parkers. I'm sure they're holding most of the answers anyway."

Ted locked eyes with Chris. "You got a problem Agent Clarke?"

"Yes sir," Chris returned. "Anytime I'm instructed to release two suspects from a crime scene of which they have been involved, I always have a problem. In particular with individuals that more than likely have information relevant to unresolved aspects of a case."

Ted Gerard set his cigar down in the ash tray. "Are you accusing me or Director Halligan of illegal procedures?"

Chris jumped in. "No sir, I just think that since we put our lives on the line to take out Alistair Krupp as well as to attempt to recover the world's most valuable violin, that all of the agents involved deserve to know just who the Parkers are and why they are so highly regarded by the Federal government".

Gerard sat up in his chair and moved in closer to his desk leaning on both arms. "That information is top secret and I am not willing or able to divulge the reason for the participation of any individuals in regards to their status, with this agency or any other."

Chris smiled a really big smile. "What about the documents sir? I overheard Jonathan Parker reading from one. Do these papers actually have any significance to our government?"

Ted gazed at both agents with a questioning look on his face. "I have no knowledge of any said documents."

"Sir…?" Chris reacted.

Gerard barked. "Subject terminated."

Chubbs looked confused and Chris was getting hotter under the collar.

Ted went back to scanning the report. "Any idea where the two suspects, Gus Happy and Maria Sanoni, are located at the present time?"

Chris continued to smile. "You might try asking your dear friends the Parkers."

Ted Gerard pretended he didn't hear this last comment. He glanced at his watch for a moment then turned his attention to Chubbs. "What about you, agent Gonzales? You've been extremely quiet this morning."

Chubbs adjusted his bulk in the chair. "Well sir, I just don't understand all of this secrecy. The Bureau seems to be denying evidence that appears to be pertinent to this case and that doesn't make any sense to me. Nor does it seem ethical if you'll pardon my inference, sir.

Unexpectedly, Ted Gerard laughed. Then he stared at his desk top for a few moments, appearing to muse over something. "Alright Agents Clarke and Gonzales, you've been with the Bureau long enough: you deserve to know as much as I am allowed to divulge."

Chris winced.

"Since the founding of this Nation, there has been and always will be certain individuals who are employed by the United States Government, who, for reasons which I am unable to disclose at the present time, have been allocated invisible status."

Ted paused to look at both of the agents. "Do either of you know about the circumstances of the signing of the Declaration of Independence by our forefathers?"

Chris smirked. "Gee, I must have stayed home the day they talked about that in school, sir."

Ted got the rub but let it go. "What the public has no idea of is the fact that our forefathers were taking a very big chance with this document. It was very dangerous at that time to express the thoughts contained within this precious article. They had almost decided to call it off when a voice rose from the back of the room and said, 'For the sake of our future sign it now!' The person responsible for this outcry could not be found." Ted took another dramatic pause. "He was one of these uniquely qualified persons who work behind the scenes and are beyond categorizing. Jonathan and Emily Parker are two such individuals. Their contribution to the security and progress of our nation is indispensible. They rest above and beyond diplomatic status. The Parkers and others like them have been serving the U.S. government for a very long time — an infinite amount of time."

Ted stood up while closing the report on his desk. "I think that about wraps it up, you're dismissed."

"But sir…" Chris was frustrated.

"I said you're both dismissed."

The two agents made their exit. Clarke turned to Gerard at the last moment. "Enjoy your golf this weekend sir."

Gerard stood behind his desk with a face of granite.

Less than five minutes later, Agents Clarke and Gonzales were seated at a table in the courtyard of Horton Plaza sipping a Starbucks double espresso.

Chris lit a cigarette.

Chubbs stared down into his coffee for a few moments then spoke. "What in the hell is going on here? We busted our asses over there and we're left out in the fucking cold on this one."

Chris noted Chubb's new found propensity for cursing since the night he took down the "man in black."

"I wish I had the answer for you bud. Whatever it is, we are definitely not part of the in-crowd."

They toasted each other with half-empty cups. Chubbs sat back in his chair. "What about these Parkers? And where in the hell are Gus and Maria? How could they just disappear?"

Chris tossed his cigarette butt onto the pavement.

"To be honest with you, I'm not sure what Chief Gerard was trying to tell us. Are there really people who live for centuries and work covertly for governments around the globe? I don't know if he's pulling our leg or what. As far as Gus and Maria go, I have a feeling that the Parkers, with their connections, managed to get them into some kind of witness program. They're probably living out of the country with new identities." Chris stared at the brown sludge lining the bottom of his cup and stood up to stretch. "I think we'd better head back to the office. It's Monday my friend, and who knows where this week will take us."

Chubbs smiled. "Copy that Chief."

Epilogue

Special FBI Agent Chris Clarke returned to his office and raised the window shade. It was turning cold and clouds were moving in, typical October weather for San Diego. He stared at the sky for a few moments and then the buzzer on his desk phone brought him back.

"Clarke here." Silence. "Hello…?" More silence. As he replaced the phone he noticed a thick manila envelope, approximately six square inches, tucked under his mouse pad. It was not there when he went for coffee with Chubbs.

He called security to see if anyone had been up to the offices while he was out. The guard reported that no one other than Bureau agents had passed through security. Chris took his pen and pulled the envelope away from under the pad. It appeared to be a high quality greeting card envelope. There was no name on the outside. He rang Chubbs. "Come on over to my office, I've got something strange here on my desk."

"Do you want forensics on this right now?" Chubbs was getting ready to push the button for chemical and explosive personnel.

Chris answered calmly. 'Nope, just come on over and let's take a look-see."

Chubbs was at Chris's door within seconds. He walked in staring at the envelope. "What do you think it is, partner?"

Chris looked up with a mischievous smile. "Let's find out."

Chris avoided touching the item in case there were prints. He used a big set of tweezers and a letter opener to carefully pry the flap of the envelope open. Inside was a card with this message.

> *Sorry for any inconvenience.*
> *Sincerely,*
> *The Parkers*

Chris picked up the card and lit it with his cigarette lighter, dropping it into the trash can. It burned up in seconds. Chubbs made no attempt to stop him.

"Well chief, what's on our menu for the week?"

"The granddaughter of a Pasadena billionaire has been kidnapped. We're up. You ready to head on out?"

Chubbs tossed his gum in the trash can. "Let's do it!"

*   *   *

ACKNOWLEGEMENTS

Special thanks go to Patricia Perez, Philippe Rhamy and his wife Tanya, Ronnie Pontiac, F. J. Dagg, and Bart Davis, for their encouragement during this project. Extra special thanks to Ken Atchity for showing me the way home.

Art Johnson was born in San Diego, California in 1945. He contracted Polio Paralysis in 1950. Undaunted by the physical restriction, he became a musician, and moved to Hollywood in 1968. As a studio and touring professional he has recorded and performed with artists such as Lena Horne, Barbra Streisand and Luciano Pavarotti. He is a Grammy and Academy Award winning participant for music. As a solo recording artist with eight CDs to his credit, he is the executive consultant for a prominent jazz record label in the U.S.

He began writing in the 1980s while working at The Philosophical Research Society in Los Angeles as one of several assistants to Manly Palmer Hall. He lectured at the Society for four years, on the subjects of Humanities and the Arts focusing on poetry and poets.

In 1990 Art returned to San Diego to become an adjunct faculty member of the San Diego Symphony. He holds an MA for music and was formerly a professor of improvisational studies at San Diego State University before moving to France in 2003. He currently resides in Monaco with his wife Patricia, where he continues to record and write.

www.ingramcontent.com/pod-product-compliance
Lightning Source LLC
Chambersburg PA
CBHW051825170626
46807CB00003B/1035